Beatitude

DJ KRIMMER

DEPRAVED
MUSES DEPT.

content and trigger warnings

Beatitude is a very dark, toxic romance.
The characters are morally black, toxic and are not a depiction of a healthy relationship. If you are coming into this hoping to find a redeeming quality in the MMC - you won't. He is a serial killer, a psychopath who has severe untreated mental illnesses. Please make sure you read over the trigger and content warnings before going into this.

Beatitude:

noun.
a: a state of utmost bliss
b: Christianity —used as a title for a primate especially of an Eastern church

Christianity

Any of the declarations made in the Sermon on the Mount (Matthew 5:3–11) beginning in the King James Bible "Blessed are"

Matthew 3:

"Blessed are the poor in spirit: for theirs is the kingdom of heaven."

For those looking for a new God—
If I can have a moment of your time, allow
me to share the word of Ronan.

contents

RONAN

PROLOGUE

Twenty-One Years Ago

"Mom! Please!" My screams echo through the sterile walls of St. Dymphna's mental institution as I struggle against the two burly orderlies. My snake of a mother sobs against my father's chest, her mascara running down her face in smudged black streaks. This is all her fault—her and that damn priest who's convinced them I'm possessed by the Devil. How can they lock me away like this? I'm nineteen, I'm a goddamn legal adult, how are they allowed to do this to me?

The old man in the cassock stands beside them, his hand resting comfortingly on my mother's shoulder as he spews out lies about their "treatment" methods. I glared at him, hatred burning in my veins. "He's in good hands." His overly calm voice is like nails on a chalkboard. "I assure you, here at St. Dymphna's, we take great pride in the treatment and curing of those who have a little more of the Devil in them than others."

The Devil? I don't have the Devil in me. I'm completely fucking fine but it's the Devil they want, they can rest assured, it's the Devil they're going to get. The priest looks at me, his eyes darkening as our gaze's lock. "You're going to be a good young man and allow us to help you, right, Ronan?"

"Fuck. You." I spit the words out, fighting against the men again. I feel something sharp puncture the skin on my ass. "God… dammit." I grit as the medication begins to weaken me, my muscles going limp, making it impossible for me to continue fighting as they strap me to the bed. My parents lean over me, tears continuing to stream down my mother's face, landing on my cheek as she whispers apologies and promises that *this is for my own good*. I glare up at her as my vision begins to blur.

"I'm so sorry," she chokes out. Sorry, always sorry. Sorry means nothing if you don't change your actions. Sorry you got beat. Sorry you spent hours kneeling on rice while praying. Sorry your father molested you while I ignored your cries and turned the music up to drown out your cries. Sorry. Sorry. SORRY.

Fuck her and fuck her sorrys. She's worse than that disgusting creature she created me with. I'm the Devil, sure. If I'm the Devil, what does that make him?

Closing my eyes, I allow the drugs to pull me into the dark abyss, my temporary reprieve from this prison. They're going to try to *cure* me, ha, good luck with that. They have no idea who they're dealing with. There is no cure for what I've become and by them holding me here against my will, it's only ensuring that once I get out of this hellhole—and I fucking will—retribution would be swift and merciless for *all* those who betrayed me.

"Bitch!" I gasp as the wretched old hag of a nun, Sister Agatha, forces the cloth over my nose and mouth once more. The holy water drenches my skin as she douses it over my face, making me feel like I am drowning in pain. My body convulses against the restraints and my lungs burn for air as she continues to chant the same phrases over and over again in Latin. She finally removes the cloth and I gasp for air, only to have her rosary viciously tighten around my neck, cutting off my air supply once again. Her cold eyes pierce into mine as she chants on.

"Daemonium!" she hisses. "Relinquo daemonium!"

"Ah," Father Martin muses while strolling into my room, his cool smile front and center. "Sister Agatha, I see you've been hard at work." He places a hand on the nun's shoulder and she releases her chokehold, allowing her rosary to loosen and air to fill my lungs once more. "Ronan, good evening my son, are you ready to have a chat with me?" It's the same question he's asked every day for a week now. He has his psychotic nun come in here and try to kill me and then he strolls in and plays the good guy. This may work on weaker people, but not me. I don't fear him, that cunt, this place or death itself. And since I fear nothing, I am unbreakable.

Staring at Sister Agatha with her gnarly yellowed teeth and heavy eyes, I sneer before spitting in her face. The deranged bitch tries to lunge at me as I laugh from my restraints in the bed. Father Martin holds her back, calmly ordering her to leave the room, as is customary.

"Hey!" I call out to her retreating figure. "The next time you wanna choke me, try going a little further south! There's definitely something down there needing to be extracted." I grin as Father Martin sighs and shakes his head before sitting in the chair next to my bed.

"You gonna tell me what the cunt is saying every day she comes in here trying to kill me?" I ask while blowing my wet hair out of my face. Father Martin's face contorts into a malevolent grin, his eyes filled with sick amusement as he continues to play this stupid fucking game with me.

"Are you going to address her by her proper name?"

"Apologies, where are my manners." I bow my head before smirking. "*Sister* Cunt."

The man's deep, rumbling laughter fills the room as he leans back in his chair, his eyes glittering with amusement. "It's a shame you're so determined to dive straight into the fiery pits of Hell," he chuckles, his voice smooth. "You've got a sharp wit, Ronan. I like that about you."

I shift uncomfortably on my wet, itchy pillow, trying to find some small semblance of comfort. "Yeah well," I begin, my voice strained from the nun's earlier assault. "I hear I'm about ten years too old for you, Daddy Martin." I wink as his amused smile turns to a dark scowl.

With a deep, guttural grunt, he slowly opens the weathered book in his lap. "Leave, demon," he mutters, his eyes scanning the pages intently. "Sister Agatha, bless her kind heart, believes there is a demon attached to your soul and is determined to rid you of it."

"Oh, how very kind," I mutter while looking at my restraints. "Tomorrow I'll make sure to vomit on her, give her a real show."

"Why do you want to die, Ronan?" His question is like a punch to the gut, unexpected and jolting. He's never asked me a genuine question before; usually, I just remind him that I know he's fucking boys in the chapel and he leaves the room five minutes later. It's disgusting really and once I'm out of these restraints, he'll likely be my first kill. Not because I'm some hero seeking justice for those poor boys; they're already broken and beyond saving. No, I want him dead because he reminds me of my own father—preaching bible verses while doling out punishments. It's a cliché, I know—always with the daddy issues—but it doesn't make it any less true.

"Now what would make you think I'd want to die, Daddy Martin?" His eye twitches at the name but he otherwise ignores it.

"You were brought here because you attempted suicide."

"Is that what they're calling it?" I breathe out a laugh and shake my head. "So dramatic I swear."

"You slit your wrists, Ronan," he states pointedly and I shrug nonchalantly—this entire conversation is boring me and I would like to get dried off.

"And your bitch of a nun seems to have a bit of an asphyxia kink, I don't see you trying to stop her from trying to kill me." The corners of his weathered lips twist in a sardonic smirk as he jots something down in his leather-bound book. I lean in closer, my voice barely above a whisper. "Do you think she's rubbing that old cunt of hers right now to my gasps and sputters while stuffing that rosary up her dry ass-cunt?"

"Enough!" he barks out, slamming his book shut. "We are

servants of God!"

"And I bet he is just thrilled to have you on his team," I mutter while leaning back. Father Martin sighs before standing up.

"You'll be dead before your thirty-day stay is over at this rate Ronan."

"You better hope so, Daddy Martin." His hand freezes on the doorknob as he waits for me to finish. "Because the second I'm free of these restraints, your bloody corpse will be laying at my feet. Tell me Father, how many Hail Mary's does one have to say to be absolved for killing a dirty priest?"

RONAN

CHAPTER I

Present Day

I've never been one who fits into society's definition of "normal." Sometimes, I can't help but wonder what life could've been like if I had been like everyone else. To not have to work as hard as I do to "blend in". To have my life all figured out like everyone in my past had expected from me. It's been a constant struggle, balancing between the person I am and the person I need to pretend to be. From a young age, my thoughts and actions have always been just a little off-kilter from those around me.

My old shrinks would dismissively label it as an understatement, then rattle off my official diagnosis. My "disorders," they called them. Borderline Personality Disorder, Antisocial Personality Disorder, Panic Disorder, a never-ending list of flaws and failures. Everything about me was deemed a fucking disorder, because according to them, I was a fucking disorder. *"Oh, your son wants to burn down your house, Mrs. Kipling? Must be something wrong with him."*

They would tell my mother with their smug smiles and white coats. No one bothered to ask me why; to try to understand the twisted thoughts that consumed me. No, I was just another damaged case that needed to be fixed. I must be fucked in the head to want the things I did... I do. Poor little me wanted to burn down the very place where my father taught me that true faith meant blindly obeying his every command... even if it meant being abused and humiliated.

Honor. Thy. Father.

Whatever, maybe attempting to burn my father and childhood home to the ground because I was forced to orally repent for making my bed wrong is a bit extreme. Honestly, maybe he saw the evil in me long before the abuse started. It brings up that age old question—is evil born or made?

The urge to give in to my darkest impulses has always been present, a menacing voice whispering in my ear, goading me toward violence. From a young age, I found myself fantasizing about harming those who've wronged me, and when the opportunity presented itself, I couldn't resist. I remember being so consumed with rage as a child. There was a time in grade school I felt my best friend deserved punishment for cheating on a math test by looking at my sheet, and I nearly choked him until he turned blue. I didn't really think much about it other than it wasn't fair that he was using me.

And then at fourteen, I nearly killed my first girlfriend during our first sexual encounter. I'll admit, that one was unjustified. I couldn't help it, my hands were around her throat and it just... happened. The rush of power was intoxicating, but my punishment after she told her parents was so severe I had to be pulled from school.

That incident taught me to hide my true desires, to only let them surface in carefully calculated moments of control. The alternative meant being locked away in a padded cell, drugged and deemed insane by society. But deep down, I know that's where I belong. And if they were ever foolish enough to release me back into the world, I would unleash a storm of carnage unlike anything seen before. Which I did after I walked out of St. Dymphna's.

At nineteen years old, I found myself trapped in the sterile walls of the ward. My scarred arms throbbed with pain as I was forced to confront my self-harming habits. It was all bullshit—I got too fucked up at a party and the guy's house I was crashing at freaked out when he saw me cutting myself. Yeah, a couple were a little deep but nothing life-threatening. It was, however, enough for me to be deemed unstable and sent away, but not before calling my emergency contacts—my parents who I had been avoiding for nearly a year.

Imagine my surprise, coming out of my high, my body restrained to a hospital bed and two familiar figures looming over me. My mother, the perfect picture of a dutiful Christian wife, kept her head bowed and her eyes trained on the ground, afraid to bear witness to anything that may challenge her twisted faith. And then there was my father, the esteemed deacon of our church, revered leader of the boys' Bible camp and Sunday school. He preached about salvation on Sundays while fucking my mouth every other day of the week until I turned thirteen. But as soon as puberty hit and I became too much for him to control, the sexual abuse stopped and the physical abuse began. Strangely, I welcomed it with open arms—it was like a gift from the God who had been forced down my throat all these years. The bruises and cuts were a welcomed reprieve from the sexual abuse I had endured. After a while, I became addicted to the pain, craving more with each passing day. I would find any and every reason to get beat just so the pain could silence everything else, even for a moment. But like with any addiction, eventually it wasn't enough, I needed more.

So, as every dumb, broken teenager does when they're looking for a release, I turned to drugs for my escape. The sensation was alright, but it left me feeling empty and dull. I couldn't stand the sluggishness that seeped into my thoughts and movements. Maybe it was years of conditioning or trauma that made me crave a sharp mind, one that could go from zero to sixty in an instant. But none of the drugs provided that release while also allowing me the clarity to defend myself if needed. It was a delicate balance, and I constantly searched for something that could fulfill both needs.

Cutting has always been my go-to coping mechanism. The sharp sting of the blade and the sight of blood dripping down my skin provided a fast and effective release from the turmoil within me. But that night at my friend's house, I was high on whatever substance I had ingested and I made a rookie mistake. The blade slipped and cut deeper than intended, leaving a jagged gash on my arm.

My hospital stay didn't improve much; between the drug screening, the multiple scars and cuts and different stages of healing and in my delirium, I may have confessed to some unsavory things about my father, but they were nothing more than fabricated lies as he and my mother tearfully argued. As always, I was just another frequent flier at the hospital, constantly shuttled between therapist offices and psych wards. My reputation preceded me—a damaged soul with no ability to speak the truth or feel remorse for my actions.

The venomous words dripped from their mouths, painting a distorted picture of innocence and victimhood. But I refused to be seen as a victim, to be pitied or underestimated. Surviving the hellhole that was St. Dymphna's was a brutal awakening, one that I didn't know I needed. It revealed to me that I wasn't alone in my darkness, that others also harbored secrets and desires deemed taboo by society. And though I would emerge from that ward a changed man, I first had to endure the wrath of Sister Agatha and Father Martin—two formidable figures who ruled with an iron fist and unshakeable faith.

During that stay, I had the same standing appointment with the Father and his psychotic nun. Every fucking day without fail. She was a devilish woman if there ever was one. She would slip into my room, drown me with holy water and try to choke me with a rosary, all while calling me a demon. She could see it in me then, the evil I was trying so hard to hide. She recommended a permanent place in the facility to the priest, stating society would never be safe if I was out there on the loose. She was partially right and as much as I hated the holy cunt, and fuck... I hated her, I appreciated her being so open with her recommendations as it showed me I had to become better at masking.

I had just slaughtered Martin; my hands coated in his still-warm blood; I turned from his lifeless body to see Agatha and, well, she was an honest mistake. Listen, don't be going around spitting nonsense about demons if you have a heart condition. I didn't expect her to come in while I was finishing off Father Martin, the old bat collapsed right then and there.

Anyhow, after their deaths, I learned quickly how to cover it up. Mind you it wasn't my best work and I'm sure I should feel some semblance of guilt for laying the blame on another patient but let's be honest, the patient was a lifer anyway and I had shit to do outside those walls.

The other thing I learned was that I can't go around killing everybody I want. I know, it should be a no brainer right? Well not for me, the itch is always there, begging to be scratched. And I had to learn that if I wanted to be on the outside, I would have to refrain from emotional outbursts that cause cardiac arrest in elderly nuns.

Like a tightrope walker, I constantly teeter on the delicate line between control and release. The slightest misstep could result in catastrophic consequences. That's why I meticulously plan and execute every move, leaving no room for error. But even in my calculated existence, I allow myself fleeting moments of liberation before quickly retreating back into my carefully constructed facade. It's a never-ending dance, this balancing act between restraint and abandon.

For nearly two damn decades, I've tirelessly honed and perfected this craft, never veering from my carefully constructed plan. It is my lifeline, keeping me afloat in a world of chaos. Without it, I would surely lose my grip on sanity and end up behind bars, or worse, dead. It is my one constant, the anchor that prevents me from being swept away by the tides of life.

That is, until now.

"Please!" she pleads for my mercy, her soft whimpers escaping those trembling lips while I revel in her agony, savoring the sight of her shivering, flawless form. Fuck, she's too beautiful for this world. Too pure for the darkness that consumes us all. I mean, who would allow an actual, literal angel to walk among us depraved sinners? And so vulnerable? It's almost laughable. But as I stare at her now, I can't help but feel a twisted sense of satisfaction. Her fiery locks cling to her pale, rain-soaked skin, highlighting every delicate curve and angle of her body. I smirk in satisfaction knowing she is mine to do with as I please, bound and exposed before me. Her once-perfect skin is marred by bruises and cuts from her struggles against the restraints, only adding to the twisted pleasure I derive from watching her suffer.

"Fuck," I mutter under my breath, trying to resist the urge to run over and lick her skin clean of blood droplets, my arousal growing with each passing second. The thought alone is enough to make my cock ache as it grows harder. I'm not usually one to draw sexual pleasure from my captives. It's not my scene and taking women is definitely not my M.O. In fact, the only woman's death I'm responsible for is Agatha, and I still fight that one.

But this sweet angel, she captivates me. She's bewitched me with her ethereal beauty and delicate nature. *How could I ever leave her alone?* My heart races with worry at the mere thought of her being in harm's way. What if I had just walked away and something had happened to her? The thought alone sends shivers down my spine. I can picture myself driving back north and suddenly hearing on the radio about a beautiful, otherworldly woman being hurt, and then finding out it was her. And had I taken her with me, I could have prevented such a tragedy from befalling her.

So, here we are.

Is my current situation ideal? No. I'd rather not have this beauty tied up in the woods, but I'm at a crossroads, it's a pivotal moment for me. I have a choice to make and it's not an easy one. I have to get back home, I need to get back across the border and head back to Canada. These are the rules. I have these rules for a fucking reason and deviating from said rules will end in my demise. Then again, I've moved so far away from my rules... what is a little more, right? Plus, I need to either kill this Angel... or take her with me. Both seem like terrible options. I don't *want* to kill her, which I know, I'm a serial killer. This should be like a typical day—walk over with a 'Hi, how are ya,' and slit her throat. But I don't want to, and not just because she's a woman. Yeah, I don't kill women, nun excluded, but if push came to shove, I would. No, this is different. She was so sweet when she bumped into me, too fucking sweet. No one is that nice, not to me. I'm a massive man with tattoos and a face that screams "fuck off". Yet she looked at me and smiled, and continued to look. No, I can't kill her.

But leaving her out here isn't an option either. If I walk away, some fucking deranged psycho could stumble upon her and do... *No, don't even think about it. It'll just put you into a blinding rage and that's not helpful in this situation.*

All I know is, her soul must be protected, either by me or I need to release it from her body. I can't allow her to continue on for one more day without protection.

"Please!" she screams again and I release a sigh while leaning against the tree, watching her petite body fight the restraints. It's fascinating how much fight she has in her. I would find it irritating in most victims, but not her. I like it when she screams. I like the thought of breaking her into submission, of silencing that fucking mouth of hers with my cock down her throat.

Jabbing my blade into the trunk of the tree beside me, I unzip the fly of my jeans, releasing my painfully stiff cock with a moan of relief. She gasps and whips around, her blindfold still tightly secured around her eyes and her arms still taught above her head. Her feet barely touch the earth while the rope creaks along the thick branch it's wrapped around.

"Please," she whispers again, and I smirk while running my hand over the length of my shaft. *That's it, keep begging.* "I-I don't have money but… I-I will give you anything, whatever it is, just please, don't do this."

Fuck her whimpers hit me in my dick as a grunt releases from inside me. It would be so easy to slip those tattered leggings down her shivering little body and bury myself in her warm cunt. My hand finds its way to that delicate throat of hers as my knife and cock compete for dominance over her quivering frame. *I wonder which would claim her first?* The anticipation drives me mad with lust as I revel in the thought of being the last thing she gets to experience before watching the light leave her eyes. I wonder what color they are. Are they blue like the ocean? Brown like the earth under our feet? No, none of those seem to fit this beauty before me.

"Fuck," I growl through a pant, throwing my head back as my balls tighten.

"Please! Sir! Help me!" She cries in pain as she stumbles, causing her shoulder to jerk because of the rope. *Fuck, I bet that hurt.*

"Ohhh god," I whimper at her panicked cries. "You're doing so good, keep… fuck keep struggling." My fist clenches with a tightness that borders on pain—but it only fuels my pleasure— as I grip my knife in my other hand and viciously stab it into the tree with each forceful thrust. In my mind, it's her soft skin I'm carving into, creating a masterpiece of agony.

"I-is that what you want?" She pants out the words through her shakes. "You need to live out some sick fucking fantasy?

Fine!" She screams while shaking her wrists.

"HELP ME!" she screams, the sound tearing from her throat with desperation. *This fucking asshole.* Can't just let me jerk off in peace, can she?

I drive my knife into the tree and stalk toward her, seizing her by the neck and squeezing until her cries are muffled and choked. But as I feel the softness of her delicate skin on my palm, a surge of twisted pleasure courses through me. *Oh my god, her throat is perfection under my hand—soft as silk, slender and delicate.* At this moment, we're connected in a sickeningly perfect way. My grip tightens as I tear off her blindfold, wanting to see the terror in her eyes as I savor the feeling of power I have over her. But as her blindfold falls and her eyes meet mine for the first time, I'm left speechless and I feel myself go weak at the sight before me.

"My god, you really are an angel," I whisper in astonishment. Her eyes—I've never seen anything like them. They're pools of shifting color, one a piercing blue that glows like frozen fire and the other, a warm amber with a single streak of her cool blue essence. The combination is mesmerizing, sending shivers down my spine as I struggle to comprehend the otherworldly beauty before me.

She chuckles, bringing me out of the trance she's put me in. "You sweet talk all your dates like this or am I just that special?" *Is she… is she being smart? With me?* No one talks with me this way. I get the screams, the tears, the begging and bargaining, but never this. No one ever looks me dead in the eyes and gives me attitude. And for her to do so while I have her tied to a tree? I give her a small smirk.

"I liked you better when you were begging and calling me sir."

"Yeah? Well, I liked you better when I was blindfolded."
I reach out, snatching her by her jaw and pulling her face to
mine. Our lips are a whisper apart as I chuckle darkly.

"Make no mistake, my sweet angel." I run my tongue
over the outside of her lips and down her jawline. *Fuck, she
tastes forbidden.* It's taking everything in my power to hold
some semblance of composure. "Your beauty may dazzle and
enchant, but it won't save you from your fate. In fact... it only
makes me savor the thought of your demise even more. I will
inhale every sweet final breath from your body, forcing your
soul into me and claiming you as my own."

Her lip trembles but her deathly glare holds firm. Leaning
in, I brush my lips against hers, but just barely. I want more, I
need more but not like this. No, if I'm going to have her, I want
her to have a running and fighting chance, and fuck, I know
she'd fight. I can see it in those otherworldly eyes.

Red catches my attention and I look at her arms to see the
stream of blood sliding down her forearm, over her small
bicep and disappearing under the cuff of her T-shirt. Before I
can administer any restraint, my tongue is on her arm, trailing
upward as the coppery taste invades my mouth. Her breath
shudders and I feel my dick hardening again, still angry over
the lack of release from before.

"Oh my god," she whispers as I move myself so my cock
doesn't touch her. I notice her gaze and stop feasting on her
ruby droplets to give her a wicked smirk.

"I think I like 'God' better than 'sir'," I tease, causing her
cheeks to redden. "You enjoy watching?" I whisper against her
ear as I grip myself and a ragged breath escapes me. "Confess
your dirty thoughts to your God, angel. Tell me, is your pussy
wet for me right now?"

"No," she spits out, her eyes filling with shame as her neck turns pink.

"Uh uhhh," I tsk while giving my cock a pull. "No need to lie, angel, it's just us here. Confess to me and maybe you'll be rewarded. Is your cunt weeping?" Her eyes flicker as that soft little mouth opens and closes several times. I chuckle as her pupils dilate. *Sweet girl, come on, confess.*

"Yes," is her meek reply. Being a man of my word, I unravel the rope from the makeshift pulley system I have and give her enough slack to fall to her knees and for her arms to relax.

She groans while rolling her shoulders and looking up at me.

"Thank you," she whispers as I grunt, my orgasm building.

"Open that sinful mouth, let me cleanse you." Shocking me completely, she obeys, opening wide and sticking her tongue out. I steady myself in front of her and while I want nothing more than to bury myself down her throat and hold her nose while she suffocates on my cock, I'm not stupid enough to think she won't try to bite my dick off if given the chance. Instead, I grip her jaw roughly as my head lines up with that tongue of hers.

"Good girl." My grunts are nearly feral as I feel my muscles tighten. "You swallow all of it. Yes, oh god look at you." I marvel as my cum coats her pink tongue while filling her mouth. I move my dick, my load hitting her face and down her neck. Dropping to my knees, I take my thumb and rub the streams over her face and neck while looking at her in awe. She stares at me, her hypnotic eyes wild, before they narrow into slits and she spits my load onto my face.

Oh, my sweet, stupid angel, it didn't have to be this way. I wipe the cum onto my hand before letting out a cold chuckle.

"Bad girls get punished," I warn as I snatch her throat and grip her jaw while shoving the cum back into her mouth. She gags and I snarl at her while roughly covering her mouth and nose.

"You will swallow it, even if it's the last thing you do." She looks from my eyes to my arm before I feel her throat bob as she swallows me. I release her mouth as she gags and shivers. "Fucking brat." A growl rises in my throat as I realize that this is precisely the reason I have no choice but to kill her. I can't leave her, nor can I take her with me. If I do, she will fight me at every fucking turn and while it's kind of cute… I think? I don't have the time for it. My plans have to stay exact, precise and it's already apparent that she thinks it's best to try and fuck with my plans. Angel or not, no one fucks with my plans. I'm about to grab my knife, turn my brain off and end this whole fucking thing when I hear it. Talking. It's far away but definitely someone talking.

Fuck, no goddamn it. This is what happens when you deviate from the plan you fucking moron. I come here, kill just one and go home. But I had to stop at that fucking coffee shop this morning, and I had to bump into her. She was so kind, so sweet to pay for me, a complete stranger, just to make my day a little happier. Obviously she's too good—too perfect for this world. I can't allow her to continue walking around this planet when she's destined for greater things. You don't accidentally bump into someone this perfect and walk away from them. I need to do it now, but… this is against my usual plans. I don't know this area on a Monday afternoon. I don't know about those who frequent the trails. And my previous victim, my *scheduled* victim will be discovered any time now on a separate trail several miles over.

"Fuck, fuck, fuck," I grit through clenched teeth while

stuffing myself back into my pants and running my hands through my wet hair from the earlier rain. My angel must hear the talking. She looks at me, those perfectly mismatched eyes wide and wild. Realization hits me in the gut.

No. She wouldn't.

"HEL-mmmf!" I slap my hand over her mouth, silencing her scream.

"Are you insane?" I snarl while looking around, listening for any change in the surrounding. Silence... everything has gone silent. If I kill her now, I have no time to erase my footprint. "Fuck!" I cry out as burning pain runs through my hand. I yank it back, leaving her lips and chin smeared in my blood. She smiles, my blood covering her white teeth and... holy fuck she's insane. I'm insane, clinically, diagnosed, committed, medicated, blah, blah, blah. *I* know insanity, and I'm looking right the fuck at it.

"I. Will. Kill. You." I grit out, trying to regain some semblance of control of this situation.

"Promise?" She spits my blood at my feet while staring up at me. Her chest rising and falling with each labored breath.

I look around in confusion before my eyes connect with hers again. "Prom—Yes! Yes, you crazy ass! What part of this is *not* screaming serial killer to you?" I frantically gesture to myself and the ropes holding her.

"Well, you seem to be doing more talking than actual killing so..." Reaching up, I cut through the rope before jerking her toward me. "I prefer my kills to be a little more private. Looks like we're going on a trip." I smirk while lifting her petite frame over my shoulder.

"Put me down!" she yells while beating on my back.

"Hey!" I smack her ass as she continues to punch me with

her bound fists. "Shut up and knock it off before I knock you out!"

"Fuck you!" she screams as I reach my car. I swear to fuck, she might be an angel, but she's acting like a fucking demon.

Opening my trunk, I toss my little hellion into the space before grabbing my syringe box out of my duffel bag and pulling out a preloaded syringe. The anesthetic is powerful enough to temporarily knock her out, but she'll still be able to breathe. I pull the cap from the needle with my teeth as she goes to scream. I cover her mouth with my still bleeding hand and growl as she bites my flesh again. Fuck, I just came and she's already stirring my cock again. This is dangerous, it's reckless and stupid, even still... it's all I can do not to climb into the trunk and consume her body and soul.

"You fucking temptress," I moan, pressing my palm into her bite as I push the needle into her neck. A tear spills from her amber eye, causing me to furrow my brows. "Shhh... don't cry, it's alright. Don't worry little angel," I coo as I push the drugs into her neck. "It's a clean needle, I would never do anything like that to hurt you. Now go to sleep, beautiful, I'll check on you soon." Her fighting begins to stop as her head lulls and her eyes begin to roll. "That's my good girl," I whisper, kissing the top of her head. Her body goes limp and starts to slump— quickly I go to catch her upper half, ensuring she doesn't hit her beautiful face. "That's my baby, sleep and have sweet dreams. I'll see you soon." Kissing her forehead again, I cap the needle before tossing it into my bag and grabbing the rope to bind her delicate wrists before shutting the trunk.

Getting into my driver's seat, I shut the car door and put my belt on while staring at my hand gripping the steering wheel, the tattoo of Sister Agatha's rosary wrapped around my wrist glaring back at me. Almost taunting me. She always told me it would happen, that the demon inside me would become too hungry and I would become consumed. And then there would be no saving me.

I would have to say, having a living, breathing angel in my trunk who has seen my face is definitely more than I ever planned to deal with. Flicking my lighter open and closed a few times, I absently pull a cigarette from my pack in the cup holder and chuckle to myself while lighting the stick and taking a deep inhale.

"What to do, Sister?" I exhale the smoke while leaning my head back.

You could let her go and move on.

"Oh could I?" I snap, rolling my eyes. "If you're not gonna help me out, you may as well fuck off." I chuckle to myself while pulling another satisfying drag from my stick. I wonder if someone looking in would think I'm insane. Sitting here, pretending to talk to that psychotic bitch.

The girl in your trunk is what will give you the insane title.

"Eh, I've had far worse in there." I watch the rain hit my windshield as I make my decision. Honestly, there wasn't ever another option, I'm going to have to take her home.

EVERLY

CHAPTER 2

As I walk into my local coffee shop, I can't help but be thankful I wore my large sunglasses as a headband last night so I can use them to cover my eyes today. I'm just not in the mood for the stares. My eyes get me a lot of head turns normally due to my extreme heterochromia—meaning my eyes are not matching in color and if that wasn't unique enough, one of my eyes is yellow, not light brown or honey, but amber yellow. It's rare and as someone who doesn't like to stand out, I hate it. Typically, I wear my colored contacts, making both my eyes brown, but since I was unable to gather any of my things last night before Devon, my boyfr—*ex-boyfriend*, decided that he's over me and changed the locks on our… *his apartment*, I have to rely on my sunglasses to hide them, along with the dark bags I'm sure I'm sporting.

"Hey, Pip!" The sweet older barista, Lucy, smiles politely at me. I'm going to miss her dearly, but with Devon kicking me out, I have nothing left keeping me here. I moved to this city to be with him since I have no family of my own and as ashamed as I am to say it, I relied on him financially. It's not that I don't want to work, I've asked Devon to let me get a job several times, but he wouldn't, stating that he didn't want me out there for other men to look at. He said I was walking sex, that my body makes men go against their better judgment and it's wrong of me to put them in that position. He would know, Devon was one of the first men to go against his better judgment and hurt me.

But because I allowed him financial control for the past three years, I don't really have enough to buy this cup of coffee, let alone support myself. Devon always said to let him worry about everything, that I wasn't able to handle bills or money. Maybe he's right, I mean, I grew up with nothing and here I am, down to my last twenty dollars and what am I doing? Buying an overpriced coffee with no phone, no car, no friends—nothing. I spent the night in a hotel that I can't afford to stay in tonight, and I have enough money for this coffee and maybe lunch. I have no idea what I'm supposed to do. Who do you talk to when you have no one and nothing? Do I go to a homeless shelter? Where are those? Would they even take me?

"Hey, Ms. Lucy, can I get my usual please." I hand her my last twenty and want to cry when I receive my change.

"No Dev today?" She asks and I try not to flinch. Devon always went with me to the coffee shop, and anywhere else I would go. Again—walking sex—I couldn't be out here alone. What if someone came along and fucked me? I swear it's only been hours since we broke up and already I'm seeing how disgusting he is. I mean, I know how disgusting he is, but I also know how cruel and dangerous he could get if he didn't get his way, so I ignored his controlling bullshit. It was the lesser of two evils and I was trapped. I should be happy that he dropped me, and maybe I am, but right now with no plan, I'm scared.

"N-No." I give her a polite smile. "Caught a cold," I lie as I move to allow the person behind me to order. But in my nervous haste I stumble over their boots and fall against them, my elbow driving into their torso.

They let out a winded "Oof" while trying to hold us steady.

"Oh my gosh, I am so sorry!" I apologize, my face going bright red while grabbing their forearm to keep from falling over them. *Jesus Everly, way to make a fucking scene.* I look up and, *wow he's beautiful.* The man I'm currently tangled over is traffic-stopping beautiful. He's tall, with messy dark blonde hair and bright green eyes. His scruffy beard adds this sexy messiness to his sharp features. He's in a black hoodie and I see the black and grey tattoo peeking out on his neck. *Is it a moth?*

"Sorry," I whisper again, releasing his strong arm as I feel embarrassment continue to flood my cheeks.

"Pip!" Lucy calls, waving me over to the pick-up counter.

"Pip," he whispers so softly I almost miss it. It's as if he's trying the name on for size, and by the look on his face, I'm assuming it's not his size. I don't blame him, I hate the nickname too, it's another Devon thing that I had no say over. As I walk over to the pick-up counter, I thank Lucy for the coffee while peeking at the man from behind my glasses. My god he's massive. His shoulders are so broad under his hoodie. I notice the silver gauges dangling in his ears and the tattoo on his hand going up to his wrist. *Is that a rosary? That's a weird tattoo.*

He orders his drink but as I glance up from his hand, I realize his gaze is on me. Even through my sunglasses, I feel like he's staring into my soul. There's the slightest upturn of his lips when the other barista gives him his total and asks for a name.

With a gentle and quiet voice, he responds with a simple "B" as he reaches for his wallet. Like a moth to a flame, I'm drawn to the softness of his tone, feeling myself gravitate towards it.

"I got this, Mason." I smile, pulling out my last bit of money to cover his drink. He looks at me, genuine shock taking over his strong face.

"What? I have money," he says, as if I'm offering him charity.

"Wha–No I'm sure you do, I was, well…it's just a kind gesture? You know, for falling over you?" I give him an unsure smile and his face still holds the same look of confusion. Laughing nervously, I tuck a lock of my hair behind my ear while sliding the money to Mason. "What, you've never done something kind before? Never wanted to make someone's day a little nicer?" I sip my iced coffee as he considers me for a moment.

"*Kindness* is not something my heart is known for, or knows of." He says it so simply, like he's giving directions but *what* he says, it's so sad. It's sad because I know exactly what he's implying. Kindness isn't something my heart knows either.

"Well, *B*, accept this as the first act of kindness on your heart." I beam brightly while placing my hand on his chest only for a second, but it's long enough for a look of near panic to wash over him. Realizing I must've overstepped, I back up a step. "I hope you enjoy your coffee and find a reason to smile today." Giving him a slight, very awkward nod, I walk out of the shop.

Once the fresh air hits me, I groan, I now have two dollars left to my name because I saw a cute guy. *So classic Everly.*

I get dumped by my boyfriend because he wants to move his new girlfriend in, so I run to anyone offering me attention. I'm not an idiot, despite what people may think. I know Devon was banging anyone and everyone willing, except me. Why would he bang me though? I'm used goods. *A disgusting dumpster* I believe were his exact words when I questioned him about our lack of intimacy. He didn't want me sexually, he wanted me to stay with him so I wouldn't tell anyone that he and his buddies took turns raping me on campus years ago. He kept me close so no one would believe me if I said he hurt me. And I let him. Maybe I *am* an idiot. I should've never gotten with him after that, but I was scared. He told me I could stay with him and he would take care of me, or he would make my life a living hell to ensure I never breathed a word about what he did. I had nowhere to go and after the attack I was so traumatized I couldn't stay at school, and I couldn't work because of my fear. Devon offered me a place to stay, and if I was living with him, he couldn't rape me again, and he wouldn't make my life a living hell, win-win… right?

I hear footsteps behind me and look to see the man from the coffee shop. "Oh!" I breathe in surprise as unease twists in my stomach. I back up against the car behind me as he walks toward me. His height and overall size are intimidating compared to my small stature and slight build. "B, right?" I give him an uneasy smile as rain begins to fall from the skies.

"Belial," his voice is still the calm, soft voice like at the coffee shop—it has an accent to it, though faint. I can't place it though. Which is shocking to no one considering up until Devon and I moved here to Oregon, I had only ever lived in a small midwest city in Indiana.

"Belial? Why is that familiar?"

"Haven't stayed up to date on your Old Testament scripture there, Angel?" He cracks a smirk and I try to relax but something in his eyes has me on edge. "It's the name given to the Devil." I frown at his explanation.

"Well, that's a terrible name to give to your child, I would go by B too, at least until I could change it." His laugh is surprised and soft, like a low rumble as he steps closer, invading my personal space.

"I go by Belial, that's not my given name, Angel. Well, I guess it *was* given to me, just not at birth. Listen, I gotta ask you something, why did you give me this?" he asks, gesturing to his cup of coffee.

"I told you—"

"The real reason," he nearly snaps but almost instantly calms back down. "Humans by nature are selfish beings, they do nothing without the expectation of something in return. Some form of gain be it financial, pleasurable or otherwise, so tell me, *Pip* what did you plan on gaining by paying for my coffee?"

"This riveting conversation." I wince as the words leave me. My mouth is always getting me into trouble and that's precisely what *Belial* is. He's all trouble. His emerald eyes darken before a smirk pulls at his scruffy face. Deciding to try and defuse whatever is igniting inside of him, I take a breath and step away from the trunk only to have him press the button on his key fob to open it. "Oh, this is your car, I'm sorry," I say while he tosses his bag into the trunk. "And I'm sorry for being a smart ass, it gets me into a lot of trouble. But you're right, I was trying to get something out of the coffee." He raises a brow as the rain starts to pick up. Wonderful, I get to walk around soaking wet as well. "I'm having a really shitty morning… day… life, I don't know. Everything is screwed up, I'm alone, homeless, I—" Shaking my head, I redirect myself. "I saw you, and something about you made me smile, even though I have nothing to smile about right now. It's probably just you're good looking, I don't know. Either way, you made me smile and I wanted to return the favor."

He's silent, my words evidently catching him off guard. "D-Do you want a ride? It's raining." I giggle at his comment.

"Yeah, I'm aware but no thank you, I've inconvenienced you enough."

"If it were an inconvenience *Pip*, I wouldn't have offered."

"You don't seem to be a fan of my name,"

"It's not your name," he states almost as fast as I could get the statement out. "Pip is not a name. No one in their right mind would look at an angel as beautiful as you and soil her with a name such as *Pip*." I feel my blush returning. Beautiful? Fuck, when was the last time I was called beautiful?

"Big talk from a man who named himself after the Devil." His chuckle is low as his green eyes nearly glow.

"Tell me your name," He states and I wrinkle my nose.

"You first," I counter while looking around. No one is out here, we're the only two idiots in the rain, perfect.

"Hmmm…Get in the car and I'll tell you." I look from him to the car. This is a bad idea.

"Taking rides from strangers is dangerous." He lets out a surprised laugh and it makes me crack a smile.

"Really? So I guess you've never used a rideshare before?" Tapping my finger to my chin I think for a moment.

"Hmm… I suppose. So do you have a rating system." He snorts and shakes his head.

"You're funny,"

"I've been called worse." I smirk before looking at his car again. "Alright fine," I relent.

"Well don't hurt yourself with all that excitement." He laughs lightly. "I do have heated seats." I'll admit, that's a luxury my frozen body would love right now. Opening the door I slide in, my body shivering as it makes contact with the cool leather seat. Belial closes his trunk before going to the driver's side and sliding his large frame behind the wheel. He pushes the button to start the engine and turns on the seat warmers.

"Thank you," I whisper, feeling overwhelmed by his presence. The sedan is average size but he takes up so much room. "I wasn't kidding about having nowhere to go though so if you want to take me to the hotel down the street, I'll probably hang out in the lobby until I'm kicked out," I half joke while sipping on my coffee.

"Sounds like a terrible use of a day," he mutters while sliding his hand down to his door pocket. Maybe he has sugar packets in there for his coffee?

"Well, I don't really know what I'm going to do yet so it seems like my only option."

"I can think of a better one." he smirks while giving me a sideways stare. I blush, figuring he's implying sex. Damn it, I should've known better.

"Oh, well…I mean I'm flattered bu—" His hand slaps over my mouth as I feel something sharp go into my neck. It only takes a moment for my body to go weak. I stare at him through my rain splattered glasses as my mind tries to get my body to fight. It's no use though. Devon was right, oh my god that fucker was right. Men are only out here to hurt me, to use me and I have no one to blame this time but myself for getting into this stupid car.

"Sleep my angel," He coos softly as my eyes grow heavy. "There's this beautiful trail a little way from here I'm sure you'll love to see when you wake up."

"Stupid, stupid, stupid," I groan while banging on the hood of the trunk with my shoe. *Perfect Everly, you happy now? You're being kidnapped and this guy is going to kill you because you got into his fucking car.* I have no idea how long I've been out this time, but I do know I need to pee and my back and arms are killing me. I feel like I dislocated my fucking shoulder from being held up from the branch while he…

I blush at the memories of his cock, his tongue and his words. He didn't scare me, not the way he should've. No, I felt challenged—alive. And I wanted so much more at that moment. *Ugh, I'm disgusting. Aroused by someone wanting to kill me? Yeah, I'd love for a shrink to have a crack at that one.*

"Let. Me. Out!" I bang in between each shout before feeling around again for the release lever. I've seen enough crime documentaries to know there should be one around here. *Enough documentaries to know about a trunk release but not enough to keep yourself from getting kidnapped.* I feel a plastic handle and pull it, causing the trunk to pop open. I nearly scream in delight until I realize he's pulling over. *Fuck, does the car alert the driver if the handle's been pulled? What a useless feature!* The car stops and deciding it's now or never, I kick the trunk hatch open before falling out and landing roughly on the road. Standing up, I waste no time, running down the nearly black, completely deserted road. *Really? I couldn't be on a freaking highway?*

I turn into the treeline and start running as fast as my sore legs will move while trying my damndest to hold my bound hands out in front of me. "Everly if you trip, so help me god," I growl to myself as I continue to run. Each stride is more painful than the last. The drugs in my system are making me feel heavy and my legs hurt from kicking that trunk. After what feels like an eternity of me weaving through trees to lose the asshole, I hide behind a tree to catch my breath. My body is shaking from the adrenaline, drugs, cold or a combination of the three—I can't see anything and my lungs are on fucking fire. My breathing stops as I hear something echoing in the distance.

What is that?

There it is again. It's a high-pitched clicking sound; like metal maybe? The sound is familiar, I just can't think of…

I freeze, the noise is right behind me, and I know exactly what the noise is—a zippo lighter. It opens and closes, again and again. Its owner sighs as they lean against the otherside of the tree. I hear them strike the lighter and the smell of a cigarette fills the air as they inhale deeply.

"Having fun?" he asks, and I nearly piss my pants on the spot at Belial's calm, almost bored tone. I pull my lips inward to stop the cry from escaping. He may not know I'm here, he could be guess—

"I can smell you," he says, still sounding bored as he takes another pull from his cigarette. "You see, when your job, your life's work, is tracking and hunting, your senses become a little more heightened. And then when one sense goes out, like sight for instance." He flicks his lighter again before coming around the tree to face me, only the small flame giving us any light source. I shrink against the tree and force myself not to scream. "Well, you know how senses work. Now, care to explain why you ran into the woods, alone, in the dark? Sweet Angel, you have no idea the type of predators that are out here. I could protect you from most, sure, but what if something came along that I couldn't fight? Or it got to you before I could? It would destroy me to watch you get hurt."

"You're fucking psychotic!" I scream out, my voice breaking. "YOU are trying to hurt me!"

"No—" His voice is sharp, like a warning before letting out a chuckle of annoyance. "No, I am saving you. I am freeing you. Freedom is not without some pain and sacrifice, sure. But what you get at the end is salvation."

"Oh my god, you're fucking nuts! Enough with your bible shit! I'm not an angel and you're no devil. You are a fucking sick, twisted man who needs help and I'm the idiot that took a ride from a stranger. There is no godly work happening."

"Godly work?" he repeats on a laugh as he puts out his cigarette. "Godly work, godly work. Tell me, *Pip, do you* believe in the Christian's bastardized version of God?" He cocks his head to one side, the glowing cherry illuminating his face just barely.

"I-I guess?" I reply nervously. Is this it? Is he going to kill me?

"Right, because of course you do, pretty young girls like you, go to church three times a year, right? Figure that's good enough but of course you also plan to marry in the church so it's fine. Dunk your two point five kids in the holy water while some old fuck who just got finished getting blown by the alter boy raises his hand to the heaven's and tells you that your children are now welcome in the Kingdom of Heaven. Meanwhile, those preaching 'god's work' are out here killing, stealing, raping. His children are starving while his flock is nestled in all safe because they give their thirty percent in order to have their spot in the clouds, sound right?"

"I-I... Belial, I don't understand! Why are you telling me this? What does this have to do with you kidnapping me? I haven't gone to a church since I was a kid!"

"You said you believe in God, think of this as his plan." My bottom lip quivers as I realize he's going to drug me again. He's going to drug me and throw me back in that trunk and... I can't. I can't do it again.

"Please," I beg weakly. "Belial, I don't know what's happened to you, if I've done something at some point to cause this but, I'm sorry—"

"Sorry?" he snaps loudly, as if the word slapped him in the face. "Sorry? Sorry?" he grits out while shaking his head. He lets out a dry laugh. "She's sorry," He mutters under his breath. "*She* is sorry. This perfect creature is sorry, to *me*."

"Belial? I-I don't know what's happening,"

"Sweet Angel, there is no God, and you aren't part of the plan." he states darkly while dropping his cigarette and stepping on it. "You and I were never meant to cross paths, then again...maybe we were." His dark silhouette cocks his head to one side, "Maybe I was supposed to find you, to help you. You're alone, homeless, penniless. Maybe your soul was calling to mine, begging me to help you. Almost as if you need me. Like I need to save you." His fingers play with my hair absently as he talks. "And I can vow to you right now, baby, I may be your damnation, but I too will be your salvation if you allow it."

"You don't know me," I grind out, my body trembling in… fear? Rage? Excitement? What is this I'm feeling? "You know nothing about me. You have no reason to keep me."

"I know everything I need to know about you." He chuckles, pinning me against the tree. "Like for instance." He inhales deeply. "That little cunt of yours is clenched so tight I couldn't get a finger in if I tried—all because you're trying to keep those sweet juices in." I shudder, shame and embarrassment flooding me at his dark whisper. His laugh is low and knowing as his hand grips my jaw and he runs his nose over my throat, inhaling me before releasing a shaky exhale. "I told you; I can smell you," He sings against my flushed skin. "You think I didn't see the excitement in your eyes when you were tied up before? I know you weren't lying when I asked you if watching me turned you on. But it's more, isn't it? Does my little angel enjoy the thought of a killer getting her off?"

"No," I spit in his face. He rears back while chuckling before grabbing my jaw roughly, his grip bruising. Forcing my mouth open, he spits into my mouth before covering it with his palm.

"Swallow," he rasps, his other hand on my throat to feel me. I swallow and he releases me roughly. "If you need to piss, I suggest you do so because this little stunt has added some serious drive time to our travel."

"How am I supposed to pee? I can't pull my pants dow— Stop!" I scream as I feel his hand on my hip.

"I'm trying to help you out, calm down."

"Help me by letting me go!" There is a long, annoyed sigh before a flashlight shines in my face. *This asshole had a flashlight and has been keeping me in the literal dark this whole time?*

"I'm attempting to be nice here. But you know what, fine. You want to go, go. Here." He grips my bound wrists and I whimper as he pulls a knife from his pocket. He flips open the blade, cutting me free. I gasp at the relief I feel upon the release. "Go on, run away. Mind you, you have no phone, no money, no car, but I'm a gentleman—here." He flips the small flashlight around and hands it to me. I'm hesitant as I snatch the flashlight from his grip and back away.

"How do I know you won't find me?" I breathe out as he grabs his lighter and steps toward me.

"Oh, make no mistake, I will," he chuckles as he slides his lighter into the front of my shirt between my cleavage. He allows the backs of his fingers to trail over me for just a second. "So soft," he marvels before pulling his hand back. "I'll make you a deal, I'll give you until sunrise to get away. If I haven't found you by tomorrow night, you can rest assured you won't see me again."

"And what if you do find me?" His smirk widens, showing off his white canines.

"*When* I find you, you will belong to me. And I will solidify this by fucking you into submission if need be." I exhale shakly as I stagger back.

"I would say no," I whisper, fear and excitement battling for control inside me. "You would be taking it without my consent."

"Would I? Because you're the one initiating the game, Angel. You don't want to play? Stop now and drop to your knees, otherwise, I'll see you tomorrow." His eyes glow in the flashlight as I look to the ground before him. He's going to find me, I know he will, and if he doesn't find me tomorrow, that doesn't mean he'll stop looking, he only said that *I* wouldn't see him again. I feel the metal of the lighter between my breasts, his silent promise that he'll be retrieving it soon. I back away, one step and then another. He slips his hands in his pockets while watching me.

"I'll see you soon, beautiful." He promises as I turn and take off as fast as I can even though I know in my gut, he's three steps ahead and already knows where to find me.

I look around the misty woods as the sun begins to rise. I'm so fucking cold, I can't stop shaking. I'm starving and I'm itchy—so fucking itchy. I've been running for god knows how long and for all I know, I'm in the same spot Belial left me in last night. Except I can't find the road, or his car. I hate that I wish he'd find me already. Last night with every snapping twig, my heart would skip. Not because I thought it was him. No, despite him giving me exactly zero reasons to trust him, I somehow do believe him when he said I wouldn't see him until after sunrise. No, I was scared because I knew the noises weren't him.

Everly you are so fucked up. I roll my eyes at myself as I keep walking. Though, there *is* some logic in finding comfort in Belial vs whatever the fuck is out here. "The monster you know" and all. At least, that's how I'm rationalizing it.

A twig snaps and my heart rate quickens, it's morning, and he is fully within his rules to come find me. I hate the excitement I feel at the thought and that said excitement is currently pooling between my legs. This man wants to kill me and yet I want him to make good on his promise on fucking me into submission.

Another twig snaps and I turn toward the sound only to be met with a hand slapping me across the face. I fall to the ground and look up in time to see a male figure—*not Belial*, grab me by my hair and start dragging me.

"Let me go!" I scream while clawing at the man's wrists. I feel something shift against my chest and remember the lighter. Reaching into my bra, I grab it and momentarily look at the inscription on the front.

"Ronan"

Shaking myself out of my thoughts, I flick open the golden lighter and strike it, the small flame ignites and I hold it to the person's hand. He lets out a wail before dropping me. I drop the lighter as I hit the dirt. I start to get up to run, but freeze. Turning back around, I quickly grab the lighter before tucking it back into my bra and trying to take off. I take too long, evidently, as the man grabs me and slams me into a tree trunk, pressing my chest against the rough bark, causing me to let out a sharp cry as the rough texture rakes across my skin.

"You come onto my property, try to steal from me and then burn me? You need to be taught a lesson," he spits out. I can smell the alcohol on his breath from last night I assume. It's stale and foul and I try not to gag while fighting against his hold.

"Let me the fuck go!" I thrash against him as he rips my

pants down causing ice cold panic to rush over me. Suddenly I'm twenty again at my college campus... "No, no, no!" I scream as he presses my face harder against the tree. "Please! I didn't! I'm lost! Please!" I cry out, tears running down my face as I feel his hand slide under my panties and grip my ass.

"It's been so long," he moans, his putrid breath making my stomach churn. I feel his bulge press against me and I cry out as he grips my arms behind my back.

"Please," I beg as my cheek rakes across the bark while he grinds against me again. I close my eyes as I hear his pants fall to the ground and feel my panties being pulled down, exposing my lower half.

"Ronan," I whisper as his bare dick slides over my ass. I don't know how I know it's Belial's name. It's not like it would be beneath him to steal something. But something tells me it is, and I pray he's close enough to hear me. "Ronan, Ronan, Ronan!" I scream as the man bends me over preparing to enter me.

RONAN

CHAPTER 3

My hunting trips always follow strict routines which are carefully planned out to ensure a smooth and undetected return home. But this time, there's a glaringly obvious factor that threatens to disrupt my plans: the beautiful glowing flag that is my angel.

I watch the man, a local woodsman, slap her across the face before roughly grabbing at her hair and I feel my anger and protectiveness flare up inside me. Every instinct screams at me to go in and rip his hands off before fucking him in the ass with them for touching my perfect girl. But as I take a step to intervene, my sweet angel surprises me once again with her fierce determination and strength. She fights back with everything she has, scratching and clawing at her attacker until she finally manages to reach for my lighter. And as she holds it up, I can't help but wonder if she's reading my name, and what she thinks of it.

My smirk turns into a cruel snarl as I watch her burn the man's hand, relishing in his cries of agony as she scampers to get away. I'm very impressed at her quick thinking, but that swiftly turns to confused annoyance as she drops to her knees, searching for my lighter. *Why? Just leave the fucking thing.* She clutches it protectively, hiding it back in her bra like some precious treasure. Before I can make a move, the man slams her against a nearby tree and his filthy hands roam over her pure body. My blood boils and I charge toward them, my control slipping away. I've had enough. I allowed her to have independence before, but now I'm taking complete possession of her.

"Please," she gasps, her voice a strangled plea that grips my heart like a vice. I've never felt this pain before. "Ronan!"

My name falling from her lips is too much. She's calling for help, *from me.* She knows I'm here; she knows I'm going to find her. She knows that I didn't leave her and she is begging for *me.*

A protective fury unlike anything I've ever felt consumes me as I charge them. I wrench the man's head back by his greasy hair and slam it against the tree trunk with all my might, over and over until the sickening crunches fade into a wet, sloppy mush. Blood sprays onto my face as I bend down and rip his belt from his fallen pants and bind his arms behind his back, dislocating his shoulder in the process. With satisfaction, I fling him to the ground and turn to face my trembling girl. My once innocent angel looks broken and bruised. Kneeling before her, I meet her tear-filled gaze, my eyes burning with murderous intent.

"You came," she breathes in disbelief. How foolish of her to think I wouldn't come for her. There is no escape for her. I will always find her.

"I told you I'd find you," I whisper softly.

"Ronan." I despise my name. It represents a past that I've

tried to forget and leave behind. The people who were supposed to love me unconditionally ended up rejecting me and casting me out like Lucifer from the Gilded Gates, damning me for daring to question the status quo. That's why I discarded my wretched name, taking on the one Sister Agatha would hiss at me before choking me with her rosary. But now, as I hear it spoken with such grace from her lips and see the look in her eyes as she stares up at me like I'm her hero, her savior... There is no name I'd rather be called.

"Everly." My eyes snap to hers as I furrow my brows.

"What?" I ask, noting the fucker next to us is coming to, not that it matters, he'll succumb to those injuries after a few agonizingly painful moments.

"My name, you asked me at the coffee shop, my name is Everly."

"Everly," her name rolls off my tongue as if it belongs there, a perfect fit for the woman before me. It's soft and melodic, like a song I've been singing for years. The syllables blend together seamlessly, it's timeless, sensual and perfect—everything she is. "Everly," I repeat, loving the way her name feels. "Such a beautiful name and you go by *Pip*." She lets out a laugh of surprise and the feeling that sound awakens inside me, it's damn near terrifying.

"No, I... Pip is short for *Pipsqueak*. It's what my boy—ex-boyfriend called me." *Boyfriend?* She has—*had* a boyfriend? A boyfriend who took her to that shop, would buy her coffee and did so regularly enough that the staff knew her by that atrocious nickname. A boyfriend who would touch those lips, look into those eyes and taste that sweet pussy. To say I'm not a fan of this turn of events would be an understatement. The thought of another man laying claim on what's mine, what was put on this Earth for me, it's enough to cause me to snap.

"Boyfriend huh?" I huff while standing up, the urge to hit something becoming overwhelming. "What a romantic nickname," I sneer while reaching into her shirt and plucking out my lighter.

"Ex," she corrects as I light my cigarette. "We broke up."

"When?" I ask before taking a long drag. I note the redness in her cheeks as she looks away.

"I don't know how long we've been ummm…in the car but, it was the night before the coffee shop." My cigarette falls from my mouth at her words.

"Three days ago?" I'm in complete shock at this. My angel, my beautiful creature has truly been put precisely in my path for a reason. It's destiny, fate, divine intervention. How else can you explain it? "You are hours from your last fuck and already getting wet for another man?" I smirk, while stepping on my fallen cigarette. "You probably still have him inside you and yet you're begging for me?"

"I never begged!" she huffs, full of indignation. "And he and I haven't in…well it's none of your business but it's been a while." *Lies.* No man would dare lay claim over her and not bury his cock inside her every fucking night.

"My pretty girl, why? Why would you lie to me? It's okay, that was before us, I can't fault you for that. But to lie about the last time—"

"I'm not lying, he preferred other girls. And there is no *us.*" I glance down at her still naked pussy, bare and singing my name. I've been a gentleman up to this point, keeping my eyes off her exposed flesh but now, now I need her. Knowing that just hours before she crossed my path, she was breaking up with another man, it fills me with an urge to take her, to consume her.

"Ronan," she gasps as I lean over her while she moves back on the large rock she's seated on. "Y-You don't have to do this." Her words come out breathy as her hooded eyes stare at my mouth.

"Don't I?" I murmur while my hands find their way up her silky thighs. "I believe I won our bet, meaning I get to claim my prize."

"But, he's…" She gestures to the twitching, garbling man who's staring at us with the one eye still in its socket.

"You're right," I state as I stand and jerk her up. "He's not going to want to miss this." I lean her over the rock as I palm her ass roughly.

"Ronan!" She gasps and tries to pull away. "We can't! He's dying and staring at me!"

"And yet," I whisper as my hand slaps her full, glistening pussy lips, causing her to cry out. "Your greedy cunt is dripping at the thought." I ram two of my fingers inside and nearly fall to my knees in worship. This woman will own me the second I'm inside her, I know it. And to think I was going to kill her. "Tell me you want him to watch as a real man fucks you," I growl while fingering her harder. "Say you like the thought of the last thing he sees is his killer fucking you senseless."

"I-I can't…" she whines while clawing at the rock, her gaze never leaving his as he fights for air.

"Oh but you will. Your pussy is going to mold to my cock so perfectly and right before he dies, you're going to explode around me, your eyes never leaving his."

"Ronan… no, I don't… Oh my god!" she screams as a burst of fluid rushes from her. I look down at the mess she's created and smirk. She's fucking sin wrapped in a saint. I waste no time pulling myself out of my pants and pressing myself against her soaked entrance. She looks over her shoulder to stare at me but I grab her hair and force her to stare at the man.

"Show him how turned on you are getting fucked while watching him die, Everly."

"Oh god," she whispers, filled with shame. I insert myself and she tries to move away at the intrusion but I grip her while ramming into her. "Fuck!" She cries out.

"You're so tight," I whimper, lifting her shirt and kissing her back. "My angel, your cunt is so tight... fuck I can barely think straight."

"Ronan," she whines my name as I pull back and push back in. I notice her gaze is on the man as her walls pulsate around me.

"That's my girl," I whisper my praise while rubbing her clit as I drive into her deeper. "Tell him, be my good girl and tell him."

"No," she growls while trying to look away. She's fighting, resisting letting go of this last strand of humanity—if only I could get her to see it's delusion, not humanity. Her mouth can spew all the lies all she wants but her body is humming another tune. I start quickly smacking her clit, causing her to scream in pleasure; she's close, I feel it. But she's not going to find her release, I won't reward her until she obeys.

"What are you doing?" She shrieks as I start to pull out. She tries to force me back but I grab her by the back of the neck and lead her to the man. Shoving her to the ground in front of his wheezing body, I kick open her legs before driving myself inside her again. I watch her as she looks from him to me and back. The shame building with her arousal. He garbles something and she closes her eyes. I stop moving and grab her throat tightly, causing her to gasp as I raise a brow.

"I'll do this all day, Angel. Now, are we going to use our words so we can find our high or do you want to keep this up?" Shaking her head, she looks back at the man and I release my hold on her, reveling in the sounds she makes as *I* allow air to flow freely through her once more.

"R-Ronan," She moans as I thrust into her. "You make me feel so—" I stop and look at her, it's her final warning.

Relenting, she looks at him and swallows, "You disgust me, you vile pig," she hisses and I slowly begin moving again. "You deserve your slow death… Oh god… and I hope you know that I am getting off on this, but it's not… fuck…" She arches her back and I feel her building up. "It's not because you're looking. It's because you're dying…you tried to take something from me, but instead I'm taking something from y-you! Shit…Ronan!" she screams my name while drenching my cock. Deciding that fuck has gotten enough of her attention, I yank her to me. Standing up I slam her into the tree as I thrust into her again and again, my eyes never leaving her glazed over ones. She whimpers with each thrust as she wraps her small hands around my throat. She begins to squeeze tightly and it's too much. I can't breathe at all as she leans forward and bites my lip.

"Watching the light leave your eyes might turn me on too." Her words are my undoing, I pin her to the tree as I rapidly release inside her, each of my thrusts more frantic and rougher than the last all while my vision starts to blacken at the edges. I grip her wrist and though it takes a little force, I remove them from my neck while breathing in oxygen once more.

"Oh, and I'm the psycho?" I pant as she smirks. It's the first time I truly see her deviant side. Her darkness I knew was hiding just below the surface. It's glorious—she's glorious, and she's mine. I lean in, capturing her lips with mine roughly. I feel her tense and she fights against me, shoving me away.

"Asshole," She snaps while standing on her shaky legs. I watch in amusement as my cum, mixing with hers runs down her thigh.

"Might wanna tuck that back in there, Angel. Wouldn't want you to lose it." She looks to where I'm gesturing and her face goes red.

"Oh my god," she whispers in shock. "I just had sex with my kidnapper, next to my dying attacker."

I take off my hoodie, leaving me in my black undershirt and hand it to her. "You say it with such regret when sixty seconds ago you were announcing me as your new God."

"Shut up!" she hisses, ripping the hoodie from me and putting it on. "So now what?"

I give her a lazy shrug before pulling my pocket knife out. I open it before flipping the blade into my hand, offering her the handle.

"When you shove it in, twist your wrist before pulling it back out, keeps the wound from sealing and the bleed out is faster."

"What?" She laughs in shock. "I-I'm *not* killing him."

"Fair enough," I state while closing the knife and stuffing it back into my pocket. "So you want to head to a hotel and get some food?" Her face drops as she scratches her head.

"What about him?"

"What about him?" I repeat while looking the body over.

"Shouldn't we... take him to a hospital or something?" I laugh in actual surprise.

"You're kidding. He just tried to rape you."

"And you tried to kill me yet here we are," she huffs and I roll my eyes.

"First off, I'ver never *tried* to kill you. If I want you dead, you're dead. Which leads me to my next point, he *is* dead. No hospital can save him, he doesn't have that kind of time. And third, even if they could save him, I wouldn't take him to the hospital because *he tried to rape you.*" Christ, this girl is as naive as she is beautiful. I have no choice, I'm going to have to protect her from everyone and everything—including herself.

"So you're just going to leave him here to suffer?"

I roll my head up to the sky. She's a lot easier to deal with when she's unconscious. "No, my beautiful creature. *You* are leaving him here to suffer. I offered you the knife and you said no. I figured you wanted to make good on what you said to him while I was fucking you."

"Ronan!" I don't particularly enjoy the scolding tone she uses to say my name. "I-I didn't...I mean...you—"

"Ohhh I see what's happening." I smirk while nodding my head. "If you don't do it, it's like he died because of me, right? Sorry, baby, that's not how this is going to work. See I don't care about him, to be fair I'm not really sure what it is that I feel about you. I mean, I saved you from getting raped and murdered... but did I do it because I care, or was it because someone else was trying to break my new toy? You get what I'm saying?" She stares at me blankly and I groan. "I'm the only one that gets to end your life. Me. Myself. Your soul, your air, your orgasms, they belong to me. Not him."

"Wow," She huffs out. "You're disgusting."

"And your pussy wept for me." I smirk as she avoids my gaze. "Listen, yes, I have a large body count, I could gut him and not think about it again. But that's not going to happen.

Why? Because you are going to do it. He tried to hurt you. I stepped in but you're finishing the job. You are not a damsel in distress, Everly. You don't need me, or anyone else to swoop in to save you. Now—" pulling the knife back out, I extend it to her once more. "End him."

"I can't," Her lip wobbles as tears roll down her scratched cheeks. "I'm not a killer, I'm not a monster. I can't do that to him, please… don't make me."

"Okay, then we leave, you get drugged—and I'm tying your legs too, this time—before throwing your ass in the trunk; and he's going to sit here, slowly dying, and that's going to be on *you*. If you would rather prolong his pain, that's on you. Again, I'm not the one putting this kill under my belt. This is your kill, you just decide if you want to remember it as fast and efficient or slow and drawn out—*cowardly*."

"I hate you," she spits out.

"I never thought otherwise, Angel. Now, what's your choice? And let me just say this before you decide. What really makes a monster? I suggested a quick end to his suffering, you, my dear are the one dragging out his pain." I smile coldly as she snatches the knife from my hand before crouching in front of the man. He's dead, he probably died when I was still buried in her cunt, but I'm not about to tell her that. I need to see what she'll do, what parts of her morality she's willing to part with. I need to know if she and I are truly halves of the same soul, and the only way to find out is to get the first kill out of the way. She doesn't need to know that it's being done on a test dummy of sorts. *See? I can be a nice guy.*

Everly grips the man's head, grimacing as she does so while…

"Everly, baby. You're going to have to use more speed and

force than that." This is almost embarrassing to watch as she tries to slowly push the knife into his neck.

"Do it yourself or shut up! I'm trying to aim!"

"Aim? It's a fucking knife! Just stab it in. You ever stab into a roast?"

"Oh my god Ronan! Shut the fuck up!" she screams, jabbing the knife into the man's neck. She lets out a gasp of surprise and I see her about to yank it out but she pauses and twists the knife before ripping it back out. She's still for several long seconds before she stands up and walks over to me, dropping the bloody knife into my hand.

"You can drug me," she says softly, "But please, no more tying me up. I can't...please?" She refuses to make eye contact with me and it's causing an ache in my chest I don't much like. Glancing at the dead body I feel something I've never felt after a kill.

Is...is this regret?

EVERLY

CHAPTER 4

W hat does it mean that I'm upset Ronan didn't drug me and throw me in the trunk? You'd think getting to ride shotgun as we head toward a hotel would be a good thing, a step in the right direction. But right now, I just want to be unconscious. I tried falling asleep about an hour ago, but every time I close my eyes, I see that man. I can still smell his blood and hear the blade entering his neck as I delivered the final blow.

I'm a murderer.

I can't believe I killed that man. I mean, sure he deserved it and had I not, he would've succumbed to his injuries that Ronan inflicted but, *I* ended his life. I stole a soul and to make matters worse, I fucked my killer-kidnapper next to that dying man before driving a knife into his neck. I'm sick, I'm twisted and demented. I'm going to Hell; I'm going to prison and then Hell and everyone at both places will know me as the whore who fucked a serial killer as a thank you for saving her from a rapist.

Looking at my hand, I see a red spot on the top by my

knuckle. "Oh my god!" I scream, while scraping my hand with the sleeve of Ronan's hoodie.

"Fucking Christ Everly!" Ronan growls, swerving the car before whipping onto the shoulder and throwing it into park. "You can't scream like that out of—God dammit not again!" He roars as I fall out of the car, but it's not to run, no, I need to vomit.

My knees hit the blacktop as I try to stand but it's too late, vomit races through me and I hurl my guts over the side of the road, sobbing in between each painful wretch.

"Oh, Angel," Ronan sighs sympathetically as he comes over and helps me stand while pulling my hair back. "Baby, you're alright." I hold on to his arm for support as I continue to wretch. How I have anything in me to throw up, I don't know.

"Y'all alright?" a male voice calls out and I stiffen while trying to finish heaving. I spit a final time before turning my head. It's another person. Another *normal* person with a vehicle. I look up to see the built man in front of his SUV. He's not as built as Ronan but still very fit under his...oh my god, that's a military uniform. I stare back at Ronan who is refusing to look at me. His eyes are straight forward and his sharp jaw ticks away. He knows. He knows I can run now and there's nothing he can do to stop me.

The man walks closer and I stand up straighter, causing Ronan's arm to drop to his side. He's not going to even try to stop me? *Is this a test?* How could it be? Ronan can't kill this man if he's in the military. He's not some no name woodsman living off the land. This man has places he has to report to and if he doesn't, people will look for him. I step toward the man and I feel a tightness in my heart.

"You okay, miss?" he asks cautiously as he eyes me up and

down. I must be a sight with my scratched face, snarled hair, lack of shoes, and pants.

"Morning sickness," I state weakly and feel Ronan's eyes on me. "Swear it's worse in the afternoon than the morning though." I give him a smile while wrapping my arms around my abdomen. The man relaxes and an easy smile pulls at his lips.

"Oh I know all about that, my wife is currently pregnant with our third. Those red and white peppermints help her when she's in the car and she starts feeling ill, I might have some in the glove box if you want some." He starts walking toward his car and I take a step, waiting for Ronan to stop me—he doesn't. I take another, and another until I'm at the man's car, out of earshot from my captor. The man comes back out of the car with a small handful of wrapped mints in his large hand.

"You sure you're alright?" He whispers, a smile on his face as he hands me the mints. "Scrunch your nose and I can protect you. I promise." My heart squeezes as my heart rate picks up. He could save me, and this all could be a horrible memory. But I can't walk away from Ronan…I don't know why, but leaving him now, like this, feels like a betrayal. It makes no sense, I owe that jerk nothing, I can't even say he saved me because if it weren't for him taking me in the first place, I wouldn't have been in the situation to begin with! Still…

"Oh!" I laugh lightly. "Because of my face? I went on a hike, stumbled and raked my face on the tree then landed in a creek! I feel so bad because my poor husband over there has been getting all kinds of dirty looks over it all day. I told him we could cut our trip short since I seem to be hellbent on messing things up but he's determined to give me one last vacation." I give him a friendly smile, making sure my nose doesn't move. "Thank you for the mints though. It's our first and I don't know what I'm doing." The man stares at me for another moment before nodding and getting into his car.

"You take care of yourself," he states and I move away as he pulls back onto the road. Once he's out of sight, my smile drops and I head over to Ronan. His eyes are wide and his jaw is slightly lax as if he's in shock by me standing here.

"What?" I ask as I pop a peppermint into my mouth. Before I can close my lips, Ronan sticks his fingers into my mouth and rips out the mint, gagging me in the process. He takes the mint and throws it against the ground before his hand grips my throat softly as he moves me so my back is against his car.

"You don't take candy from strangers, Angel." I roll my eyes which seems to annoy him further. "Okay fine, you don't take anything from another man. It's bad enough you walked over there in nothing but my hoodie."

"And whose fault is that?" I snap back, causing him to lean in, his lips just a breath from mine.

"Next fucker to offer you a hand, loses it. Now get in the fucking car," he grits out. His eyes betray him though. He looks nervous, confused but also relieved. His jaw isn't as tense and his eyes aren't as dark. Why though? Why is *he* nervous?

I slide my foot into the car as he releases his hold on my neck to allow me to take my seat. He closes my door and walks around to the driver's side, getting in before putting the car in drive and taking off down the road once more.

"You didn't leave." His voice is soft and almost timid. It's unnerving coming from him.

"You won the game," I reply softly while looking at my hand, the blood spot is gone, but it's like I can still feel it. Using my nail, I scratch at the spot, trying to make the feeling go away.

"Don't bullshit me," he snaps while whipping into the parking lot of the hotel. I'm shocked, it's actually a nicer looking hotel than I thought he was going to take us to. I don't know why but I saw a by-the-hour room in my future.

"Ronan, I can't go in there like this," I say while gesturing to myself. Ronan looks me over and shrugs.

"Stay in the car then, I'm going inside and taking a shower."

"You're going to make me walk in there, filthy, with no pants or underwear?" A small smirk pulls at his lips as he stares at my lap before frowning.

"What are you doing?" He asks, gripping my hand and jerking it to him. I look to see I've dug at my skin so deep I'm bleeding.

"I had an itch, I wasn't thinking."

"Why didn't you leave me?" He asks again while reaching in his glove box and pulling out a tissue pack.

"Because I couldn't," I whisper as he pulls the tissue out and dabs at my scratch. He's so gentle it's almost unnerving. This man is a killer, right? Why is he fussing over my scratch?

"You could've," He says, though he seems distracted as he reaches back into the glove box again and pulls out a tiny first aid kit. "You're an attractive woman, and you told him you were pregnant. I watched his protective side flip on. I know he asked you to give him a sign if you needed help. He could've gotten you in the car and drove off before I could've stopped him. So why did you stay?" He places a bandage over the scratch as his green eyes bore into my soul.

"You asked me not to," I whisper, my gaze falling to his mouth.

"I never asked you anything,"

"I felt it," I swallow before touching my chest. "Here, I felt something. And I think it was you, begging me not to leave you." His earlier words hit me and I reach out with my hand and touch the side of his face. The act seems to almost scare him and as he flinches away, I repeat his words. "It was as if you needed me. Like I'm needing to save you." His eyes look almost fearful as he looks down at my hand.

"If that's really what you think, Angel," He shakes his head before opening his door. "Then you should've dove into his car when you had the chance."

RONAN

CHAPTER 5

I inhale deeply, watching the red tip at the end of my cigarette glow as I rest on the balcony of the hotel. Usually I prefer things a little more lowkey. Not a roach motel or anything, the last thing I want is to be sleeping on someone else's dried fluids or end up with bed bugs. But a suite with a balcony overlooking the mountains isn't something I'd splurge on if it were just me.

She's special though, and despite having to lock her ass in the trunk a couple of times, I do want to show her some semblance of niceness. Especially after earlier…

What was that? She could've left and there's no way I would've been able to stop her. Now, it's true that I would've eventually found both of them and after taking back what belongs to me, I would've crushed that fucker's skull with my boots. But she didn't know that. She chose to stay; she lied without hesitation. She says she felt me begging her not to leave. I want to say it's a ridiculous notion that she felt some sort of otherworldly connection causing her to sense my thoughts and feelings after only knowing me a few days. Or it would be ridiculous if it weren't exactly what happened.

I was begging her. I don't beg for anything. I learned a long time ago that begging didn't help and only showed your weakness. But for her, I don't think there's anything I wouldn't do for her. I stood on the side of that road, staring into the woods while silently pleading that she wouldn't run again. I didn't want to lose her, I didn't want her to get in his car and to leave me, all alone. Funny, I always preferred to be alone but the thought of not having her heart beating in the same vicinity as my own... It's enough to drive me insane.

So I did, I mentally pleaded: *Please, please, please, Everly... don't do it, don't leave me alone. Don't make me chase you again.* I would've in a heartbeat, make no mistake. But in all honesty, I'm fucking exhausted. And throwing that man around and beating him to death, I'm still recovering from it. My body is sore and aches far more than it used to.

Flashes of that fucker bending Everly over flash into my head. I was almost too late, a moment longer and he would've...

I hiss as the hot cherry hits the top of my hand. Looking down I see I've snapped my cigarette in half. Sighing, I absently flip the lighter open and closed, enjoying the sound it makes as I try to tamp down the rage inside me. I've been told I'm cold, lack emotion, empathy, whatever. It's not true. I actually feel very deeply, deeper than most if I'm honest. But I only feel it about certain things. Animals for instance, I love them. I care for them and I have killed to protect them. People? Not so much. I find them to be selfish, loud and predictable. I need humans for two things—fucking and hunting. Or I did.

The knocking on the door pulls my attention and I go to answer it just as the hotel employee drops the bag on the floor. Picking it up, I lock the door and turn, nearly running into Everly. My god, it amazes me how frequently this girl manages to steal my breath.

"Who was that?" she asks, clutching the green robe around her bare body.

"I got you some clothes," I state, my voice thick. I hold up the bag and see the appreciation on her face. It makes me itchy. Now that we're not in danger or she's not screaming for her life in the trunk of my car, I feel like she's going to see me, the real me. Not Belial the serial killer. But Ronan Kipling, the awkward guy who never fits in, the guy who fumbles over his words because his brain moves a million times faster than his mouth. The idiot who is staring at her, unable to figure out his next move and it's putting him into a near panic attack.

"Thank you." She smiles, taking the bag. "Really, I appreciate it, I wasn't sure what I was going to—"

"Shut up," I state, pressing her against the wall. Her eyes go wide as my hand wraps around her delicate throat.

"Ro—"

"Shut. Up." I grit out while trying to think. This is too domesticated. I can't do something this normal. Even with someone as beautifully perfect as her, it can't be this way. I slip my hand over her bare chest and under her robe.

"Please," she whines out as I brush my fingers over her nipple. "Please, stop." She pants as my hand continues to knead her breast while my left hand slips lower, finding its way to her pussy. Slipping a finger in between her lips I feel the wetness and raise a brow.

"Your mouth says stop but your body is vibrating with the need to be touched. So which is it, Angel?" I untie the sash on her robe before unveiling her tits and my fucking god. I fall to my knees as I suddenly feel unworthy to look at this creature before me. As I look from her tits to the delicate curves of her body I pause and frown at the thin scars along her hips, they travel over her thighs as well. Reaching out, I allow my fingers to touch a slightly thicker white scar.

"S-Stop." Her voice is far more forceful this time and as I look up to meet her gaze, I see the shame and anger on her face. "Just stop, okay?" She goes to pull away, closing her robe but I grip her arm. She snatches it back as I stand and grab her neck.

"Let me go!" She yells and I grip her, slamming her onto the bed while reaching into the bag and pulling out the underwear I ordered and stuffing them in her mouth to shut her up.

"We are in a nice hotel," I warn, my voice low as I rip off my belt and wrap it around her wrists. She shakes her head violently as I do so, tears spilling over as her sobs are muffled.

"I'm sorry, baby," I coo, stroking her cheek. "I know you don't want to be tied up, but you won't stop fighting me. What other choice do I have?" Her glare is a deadly one I'll give her that. Leaning over her, I go to give her a kiss but she jerks away and tries to say something—the panties muffling it. It sounds like an "I hate you" but who really knows.

"I told you," I hum while running my finger tips over her abdomen, causing goosebumps to erupt over her bare flesh. "You should've dove into that car. Now, be a good girl while I shower and when I come out, we can talk about removing the belt and maybe get some food, okay? Would you like that?" My words are laced with false sweetness as I eye her scars again. She takes her leg and kicks me as hard as she can against my hip.

"Fuck," I laugh out while rubbing my aching side. "Such a little fighter. Be a good girl for me, I'll be back." I smirk at her muffled screams as I turn and head toward the bathroom.

It's still steamy from her shower and I see the smiley face she drew on the mirror. It's sweet, innocent and not at all what I would expect from a woman covered in so many scars. Removing my clothes, I turn the shower on and step in. As I stand under the hot water, my mind wanders to my own scars. The deep ones inflicted by those who wanted to hurt me, and the more shallow ones I created in moments of desperation. My need for release was what initially drove me to this life, before I found my true calling in this game. And now, with my body decorated in intricate tattoos, it's been years since I've felt the urge to cut myself open for temporary relief.

As I finish up in the shower I can't help but wonder, how long has it been for my angel? Looking at the smiley face again, I walk to the mirror and draw a heart around her drawing and a halo over its head before walking out of the bathroom.

"You ready to talk about dinner?" I ask while rounding the corner and drying my hair with a towel. I look at the bed and my heart stops, it's empty. I hear something and go to turn when someone jumps on my back and I feel something sharp pierce my skin. Everly jumps off me, one of my now empty syringes in her hand.

"Oh—" I laugh lightly as my body grows heavier and I begin to stumble. "You...fucking brat." I stagger to the bed, falling onto it as the room begins to spin. I feel pressure and watch as Everly appears on top of me, straddling my waist.

"Baby, I hate to tell ya," I slur while trying to fight the drugs coursing through me. "But my dick is going to be as unconscious as me in about sixty seconds."

"While I can do a lot in sixty seconds, I'm not going you to fuck you." She leans in and grabs my jaw roughly before gripping my bottom lip between her teeth and *fuck yes baby, bite me.*

I groan as the metallic taste of my blood fills my mouth while I try desperately to kiss her back as roughly as she is me. It's no use though, my muscles are not cooperating.

I chuckle against her mouth; she may say she isn't wanting to fuck but that slick cunt sliding over my stomach begs to differ.

Everly pulls back, my blood staining her pink lips as she watches my eyes roll.

"What are you gonna…do?" I murmur, my eyes refusing to stay open.

"Well for starters, I'm going to tie you up, and then…" She leans in and licks my ear before whispering, "I'm going to kill you."

"That's fine," I mutter weakly. "Just keep rubbing that cunt on me… while… you do."

"Right there," Everly's small whimper breaks through my drug induced sleep. *How long have I been out for? Fuck my head is killing me.* Does she get headaches when I drug her? If so, I may have to apologize.

"Mmmm…" I groan, feeling something around my dick. Fuck it feels so good. I open my eyes and try to focus as

Everly's body comes into view. It's dark in the room, only the lights from outside are allowing me to partially see her. Her tits bounce as she roughly moves up and down my dick. "Fuckkk…" I growl, trying to move my hands. I'm trapped though, and not by my belt. No, she's apparently rifled through my bag and found my fucking handcuffs. "Ohh," I laugh to tamp down my anger. "God when I get a hold of you…Fuck!" I hiss in pain as she rakes her nails down my chest.

"I was gonna kill you," she whimpers, grinding her clit on me. "But I thought of something better. I'm going to get even with you instead," she pants and fuck if she thinks I give two shits what she's talking about while her cunt contracts around my cock, she's wrong.

"Baby I got an idea," grunting, I buck my hips up roughly to fully impale her, causing her to scream in pleasure. "How about you shut that fucking mouth before I do it for you." I begin thrusting faster and it's as if she knows I'm nearly there. An evil smirk forms on her face as she rolls off me.

"Oh fuck no!" I snap while pulling at my restraints. She laughs while walking over and licking her arousal off my cock before spitting it on my chest.

"Now, my date is going to be here soon." She smiles while slipping on the panties I bought her. "Don't worry, he likes an audience." The murderous rage I feel pumping through me is unlike anything I've experienced before.

"You let someone else touch you, *anywhere* and I'll kill them, Everly," I growl out my body vibrating. "Make no mistake, his blood will be on *your* pretty little hands." She raises a brow while swinging her hips as she walks to the edge of the bed.

"Awful big talk for a man cuffed to the bed,"

"You vomited after you drove my knife in your attacker's throat, you think you can handle another. And this fucker will be innocent." I warn, the growl low in my chest. She leans over me, her hand rubbing her spit into my tattooed chest.

"You still think I'm an angel?" She grins as her hand grips my balls.

"Fuck!" I hiss through a chuckle. "Yeah," I pant out as her hip tightens, causing the pleasure to go into uncomfortable territory. "Yeah, I do. Though of course, Lucifer was once God's most loved angel before he pissed his father off." The warning undertone isn't lost on her, but she doesn't care. Everly is drunk off the power she's feeling right now and it might be the first time I actually feel like someone is capable of killing me. The fact that my cock is starting to grow harder again at this revelation confirms that I am, without a doubt, fucked in the head. Eh, that's alright.

"Ohhh… so I'm Lucifer now." She smirks while roughly biting my nipple.

"Fucking shit!" I groan, my cock screaming to be touched.

"Does that make you God?" she whispers against my ear while tonguing my ear gauge.

"*Your* God, yes." I rasp out. A light tap on the door grabs our attention and I feel my heart hammering as she pulls back to stare at me with her mismatched eyes.

"Well, *Daddy God*, get ready to cast your naughty angel out of the pearly gates."

"Everly," I warn as her grin grows wider. "This is your last—" She slips her panties back off and stuffs them into my mouth before slapping my cheek teasingly. *I'm going to kill her. I'm going to kill him, and then her.* She's unhinged and on a level I can't even fathom. She's chaos. What was I thinking?

She's no sweet, innocent angel. She's a depraved deviant who wants to watch the world burn. I watch in fury as some nameless tall man walks in, his eyes not leaving *my* girl's bare pussy which is on full fucking display for him.

"Fuck—" he smirks, licking his lips. "When I answered your ad I thought for sure this was a scam." Everly stands at the foot of the bed as the man walks up behind her. His hands touch her bare body and I growl through the underwear while yanking on my cuffs. He looks me over nervously, he should be nervous because I'm seconds from inflicting the worst kind of pain on him. "You sure he wants this?" His laugh is full of apprehension as I glare at him, silently promising him death the second I'm free. "He looks…kind of angry." My response is an audible exhale through my nose as I continue to stare holes through him.

"Of course," Everly lies, my fucking angel is starting to prove to be very good at lying. Her eyes never leave me as she leans against the man's unimpressive chest while guiding his hand to her cunt. "Look how big he is, if he didn't want this, you think I could've got him in the bed and cuffed him—Oh!" I scream through the fabric as his hand soils her by touching her clit. She looks me dead in the eyes while releasing a pant and grinding against his hand. "Right there," she whimpers, rocking her hips.

I don't see red, it's just white, white hot rage. I hear his zipper and watch as he pushes her to bend over on the bed and I've had enough. With everything I have, I slam against the bar on the headboard that I'm wrapped around. It takes three tries before the post gives way. I'm up in an instant grabbing the startled man and slamming him against the wall while removing the underwear from my mouth.

"No one touches what's mine." I growl out before grabbing him and snapping his neck. His body crumples to the floor and I step over him, walking back to my girl who is on the bed, hands over her mouth. I stand before her, my breathing labored, my body vibrating with adrenaline and a rage unlike anything I've felt before. In a swift motion, I wrap the chain from my cuffs around her throat and tighten my hold. She sputters while trying to grip the chain in a futile attempt to loosen my grip.

"Why are you so disobedient?" I grind out in frustration. "I got you a nice room, I was going to get us a nice dinner, I bought you clothes and *this* is how I'm thanked? Why? Why do you enjoy making me snap?" I release her before stepping away as she coughs and gasps. What am I going to do? There is a dead man in our room. An unknown, *very dead* man.

"You're a fucking psycho!" Her raspy voice screams as she hurls a pillow at me. I stare down at it and almost laugh. It's such a silly thing to hit a killer such as myself with. "A vile, moral-less, psychotic monster!" My eyes flick from the pillow back to her.

"And your cunt is weeping for me," I smirk as her eyes shudder. "You brought a stranger in here and allowed him to touch you, just to see if I would stop him. You enjoyed it, didn't you?" She opens her mouth and I see the lie she's about to allow to spill, I give her a warning look and she snaps her mouth shut. "That's what I thought. You get off on this. On murder, danger, jealousy, don't you?"

"I…" Her voice is so small and full of shame. I don't like it. Yes, a dead man in our room is less than an optimal situation but I'll figure it out. There's no room for shame though.

"Never turn your gaze toward the floor as if you're

unworthy," I spit out. "If this is what you want, you better own it."

"Ronan," she whispers, it's a weak plea and I shake my head.

"Everly, if you want this, prove it. Leave that shame over there, get on your fucking knees and crawl to me. Come here and finish what you started." She hesitates and looks at her bed as if I'm actually giving her a choice. It's cute she believes it. One day she'll understand that we will be together; even in death, our souls will intertwine, both halves of the same soul, bonded together once more, a twin flame. I refuse to let her leave. But, I will allow her the illusion of a choice, as long as she chooses correctly.

Everly slides off the bed and onto the floor. She looks up at me as she crawls on her hands and knees, her ass bouncing with each move. She stops in front of me and I reach down and stroke her hair.

"Such a good girl," I praise as she nuzzles her cheek with my hand. She reaches to free my cock from my pants but I stop her. "Put your hand in your cunt. Show me how wet you are for your God." Everly reaches her hand down to her pussy and whimpers as she touches herself. She pulls her hand out and I release a moan at the sight of her glistening juice coating her small hand. Walking over to my bag, I pull out my hunter's knife and walk toward her. She flinches as I raise the blade and only calms once she sees I've inserted it into our dead friend's abdomen. "Put that cunt on that handle and suck my cock. You don't stop fucking or sucking until I tell you to, understood?"

Everly nods before straddling the man and crying out as she inserts my handle inside her. "Fuck," she whimpers while looking up at me. Her cheeks and chest are red with arousal and her eyes are hooded and glazing over.

"Fuck is right," I rasp while freeing my cock. I grip the back of her head, ramming my thick length down her delicate throat. I give her no time to adjust or recover as I pull out and slam into her again. "Start bouncing," I grit between thrusts. Everly is gagging, drooling and tears are running down her face and chin. She listens though. Of course she does. My sweet, perfect angel slides up and down that long handle, gasping and whimpering around my cock as she does so. She looks up and our eyes connect and fuck, in this moment, I feel like I must've died and gone to Heaven. Her inner thighs as smeared with that fuckers blood and she shivers as her eyes roll back, an orgasm taking over.

I rip my cock from her mouth and drop to my knees. "Spin," I pant out. She cries out as she spins around, now face to face with the dead man, her cunt still sliding up and down my handle. Bending her closer to his chest, I spit on her ass and slip a finger in.

"No!" She gasps at the intrusion and tries to pull away.

"Finger that clit." I grunt thickly. "*Now.*" She whimpers but does as she's told and it's not long before her legs start shaking and she arches back crying as she releases her fluids, drenching my knife. I rip her off the handle, collecting her arousal in my hand and lubricating my cock before pressing the head inside her ass.

"Ow! S-Stop!" She cries again as I invade her. "Oh fuck… mmm…"

"I won't," I nearly whimper as I pull out and ram into her. "I will never stop, Everly." I growl between each thrust as I encircle her with my cuffed arms and guide her back to the blade's handle, but this time, I'm in charge of her clit.

"Ronan!" she cries, coming again as I drive faster into her ass. She leans forward, as if too tired to stay up and I pinch her clit roughly before smacking it rapidly. "Oh god," she whimpers as I lick the sheen of sweat off her back.

"Yes, my sweet Angel," Panting, I roll my head toward the ceiling as my balls tighten.

"Ronan…d-don't stop," she grunts before coming again and it's my undoing.

"Fuck!" I roar, burying myself deep within her ass as I release. My body shudders as wave after wave of please rolls over me. Removing myself, I smirk at the small cry escaping her. "You can—" I inhale, steadying my rapid breaths. "You can stop now, Angel."

Everly removes the handle and goes to stand but her legs give way. "Hey, hey," I coo, pulling her into my arms. "Easy there sweet girl," I carry her to the bathroom and turn on the shower before walking to my bag and rifling through to find the keys to my cuffs. Once free, I return to her. "Let's get you cleaned up."

"What did I do," She whispers, her body shaking as realization floods her. Her eyes find mine as I help her into the shower. "I killed another man."

"Technically *I* killed him." I smirk while leaning her back under the water.

"I brought him here, I killed him and…oh my god…" She wretches while shoving past me and leaning out of the shower to hurl into the toilet.

"Everly," I groan out. "Baby, you gotta stop puking every time someone dies." She glares at me while straightening and shoving me against the wall. Deciding to be a nice guy, I fall against the tile and let out a grunt for added effect.

"You're a monster," she hisses, her voice laced with venom.

"I am," I agree, my eyes trailing over her curves as the water streams over her, washing away all evidence of what transpired out there.

"You disgust me," she spits and I smirk.

"I should,"

"Stop agreeing with me!" she huffs and her foot slips, I snatch her arm, holding her steady against my chest.

"I will stop," I whisper, running my hand through her hair. "When you say something I don't agree with. I know what I am, Angel. I know I'm unhinged, unwell, I know..." I chuckle lightly, though it's void of any humor. "I know I'm a monster, a psycho, a demon...a freak." I grit out as flashes of my childhood and teen years flood me. The water hitting my skin makes me flinch as memories of Sister Agatha drowning me in holy water surfaces.

"Unclean," I grit out, my hands gripping my head while it feels like there's a crushing weight pressing down on my chest. *Unclean, unclean, unclean.* I'm filthy, a sinner, a vile sinner who must confess his sins to his father, to be absolved. To be saved.

I was never saved. I was a good boy; I did as I was told and it didn't stop.

I see the tattoo of Sister Agatha's rosary on my hand and I feel her tightening the strand around my neck, it's my undoing.

"Ronan?" *Everly?* She was next to me but I can't see her now, I can't smell her. I'm drowning.

"Ronan!" Something touches my neck and I snap out of my haze. Instinct takes over, I grab it and twist before slamming the figure against the wall. "Ronan stop," she cries out and I blink, seeing my angel's wide, fearful eyes.

"Everly," I whisper as she touches my face, causing me to flinch.

"Shhh…" She coos, putting her other hand on the other side and stepping closer. "You're okay," My breathing is still labored and I'm shaking beneath her hands. Her concerned eyes search mine. "Where did you go?"

"Somewhere I should've stayed." I manage over the lump in my throat. "You're right, I am a monster…"

"I know," she admits while turning the shower off. "But so am I, and even monsters deserve some semblance of happiness, right?"

"Everly," her name is a shaky plea as I feel myself becoming too heavy. "You're no monster, but if you stay with me…you'll become one." Looking away, I step out of the shower and grab a towel. I want her to stay, and every part of me is screaming to keep her. And I will, but from afar. I will let her go, but she will never be free of me. And I… God, I will always be hers.

"I'm going to get this cleaned up," I state, my voice hollow and distant. "There's ten thousand in cash in my bag, take it and go. Our adventure has come to an end."

"What?" She squeaks out while stepping out of the shower, her skin rising in goosebumps from the temperature change. "I've killed two people in twenty-four hours! There's no going back, Ronan."

"You've killed no one," I huff dryly. "I killed him and the woodsman was dead while I was still fucking your brains out. I just wanted to see what you would choose."

"Why?" she asks as I continue to stare at the tiled floor.

"I don't know, morbid curiosity? I told you," I tap my temple roughly. "I'm fucked up."

"No." She states firmly, walking out of the bathroom with

me following her. "I refuse to believe that you did this out of boredom. I didn't believe you at first but… but Ronan, you and I, we are something. You know it, I know you feel it."

"What I feel," I glare at her while curling my lip. "Is boredom and annoyance. Now take the money and get the fuck out of here."

"No," She straightens though her voice is shaking.

"Get out!" I roar causing her to cower slightly, but she doesn't make a move for the money or the door. Fed up with her defiance I march over to the bag and grab the banded bills and hurl them at her feet. "You take that fucking money, and you get the fuck out. I'm done with you."

"Well I'm not done with you!" she snaps, taking me by surprise. *Not done with me? I am the monster who drugged her and wanted to kill her, I still might…what is she talking about?* "And fuck you by the way," She hisses, while hitting me with the money. "We go through all this and you hurl ten grand at me and say have a nice day?"

"It's all I have on me," I mutter, still trying to wrap my brain around what's happening. "Is that why you're staying? You want more?" Well that's a look of rage I've never seen on her.

"I will cut your tongue out of your fucking mouth if you say something like that to me again! I don't want your money or anyone else's you fucking prick!" Raising a brow, I reach in the bag and pull out my pocket knife. I open it and flip it to her.

"Well, go on then Angel, do it." She takes the pocket knife as I drop to my knees.

"What is the matter with you?" She whispers softly as I close my eyes.

"Better idea, take that knife and fucking drive it in me. All I ask is I get to see your eyes as I leave this world."

"Ronan," she grabs the back of my head and I let her take control. It's so unnatural to give up the power, but for her, I'd give her anything, everything. *Take me out baby and run away. You'll never have to look over your shoulder and wonder if I'm there.* I hear her drop to her knees and I open my eyes, watching my blade go to my throat. I stare into her heavenly eyes and give her the slightest nod. She pushes the blade against my skin and I feel the bite of the blade. I welcome the burn and release, it's so freeing, and I know any second, I'll never have another thought or worry again. I look at my sweet girl, making sure she's my last vision, my last thought, my last prayer. My final heartbeats belong to her and only her.

Everly pulls the knife from my throat and closes the blade. I'm about to ask her what she's doing when her lips are on my neck where the blade had been. She runs her tongue over the cut, lapping up the trail of blood.

"Fuck," I whimper, having to force back a rouge sob trying to escape as she moves to my mouth. I taste the copper from my blood and growl while fighting with her tongue over dominance. Gripping the back of her head I yank her from my mouth and stare at her in bewilderment.

"Why?" I ask weakly. *Fuck please, make me understand.* Why? Why is this beautiful creature holding me instead of ending me?

Her delicate fingers trail over my rough, stubbled cheek as she whispers my name. The warmth of her touch melts away the darkness trying to pull me under. "Even the monsters need love,"

"You can't love a monster," I choke out, regurgitating the line I've had drilled in me since adolescence. Everly climbs on my lap and holds me in place.

"You can, if you're a monster too." Her hand grabs mine and I feel the raised areas of skin on her thighs. She's letting me touch them. It's what started the whole night's events, me touching her scars.

"You aren't my first kidnapper, let's just put it that way." She admits and my hand twitches, gripping her thigh as I glare at her.

"What?" I grit out, my mind unable to focus on anything except for the thought someone had hurt her.

"Parents didn't want me; I was in the foster system which was its own treat. I ended up getting a partial scholarship and working to go to college,"

"What happened?" Her mouth twitches and she gives the smallest of shrugs.

"Group of college guys took me to some shack, drugged me and kept me for a weekend. Took videos, photos, they… they ruined me. Then they went back to school like nothing happened."

"That makes them the monster, not you." I say while running my fingers through her hair. "Who were they?" A small dry laugh escapes past her lips.

"I don't know them all, but one was my now ex."

"Your ex as in *Pip*." She nods softly, not meeting my gaze.

"Devon," She says his name and I grab her, pulling her in for a rough kiss. She whimpers as I pull her tongue into my mouth and suck the length of it before sucking on her upper lip and then her lower.

"Never soil your perfect mouth with that name again." Her eyes are wide as she stares at me, her swollen lips parted as soft pants escape. "Say the word and I'll kill him." I whisper even though she doesn't have to say a word, no this fuck was already on my shit list for touching her, but knowing that he attacked her…he's dead.

"Gonna be hard for you to do anything if you want me to kill you." She whispers against my mouth as her hand runs over my cock.

I growl possessively against her mouth, "I'll figure it out, don't you fucking worry. He's a dead man."

"Can I tell you a secret?" she whispers while nipping on my jaw. Fuck this feels so good.

"Mhm," I moan while closing my eyes, enjoying the feel of her.

"I like that you don't want anyone to touch me."

I peek open one eye. "No one is worthy enough."

"But you told me to kill you, if you're dead, someone else might have to touch me." I snatch her by her throat and bring her to look me in the eyes.

"*No one* touches you, except me." She grips my throat and gives me the same intense stare.

"Then you better stay the fuck alive. Because you die, and I'm fucking any and everyone just to piss yout off." She smirks and I snap. I'm up in an instant, slamming her into a wall while gripping my cock and slamming it inside her cunt without warning. She releases a sharp cry at the intrusion but I don't care. Walking outside onto the balcony, I set her on the metal railing and she gasps as I lean her over it.

"Ronan!" she cries as her arms hold the railing with everything she has as she hangs upside down. I ignore her as my fingers dig into her thighs, while I fuck her deeper and harder. "Ronan! I'm going to fall!" She cries through her moans.

"If you fall," I grunt between thrusts. "I fall with you, Angel.

You're right, I can't leave you in this world, and I can't be in this world without you—fuck!" I roar, tossing my head back. She screams as her hands slip but my hold is firm as I grind her clit against my pubic bone. She screams again, this time out of pleasure as she releases, I pull back as her fluid rushes from her center. "You're so fucking perfect," I grind out, ramming into her again and again as her walls tighten around my pulsating cock. "Such a good girl, so fucking drenched. Right there, Angel, that's it, tighten that cunt around my cock, fuck…Everly!" Crying out, I slam into her rapidly as I shoot my load deep inside her quivering body.

Once I finish, I pull her up and when I do, her eyes roll and she goes limp in my arms. "Sorry, Angel," I smirk, kissing her head. "Guess I took too long."

EVERLY

CHAPTER 6

Groaning, I open my eyes, my head throbbing. Looking around the hotel room, I note the almost too-clean smell. Not what I'd expect considering there's a dead man on the floor. *Fuck, a dead man.* What is the matter with me? How have I allowed it to get this far? What am I doing? I've been responsible for two deaths in as many days and why? Because I get off on a possessive killer wanting me? I shouldn't be this way. It's sick. I know it is but, I crave Ronan more than I crave my next breath. It's something I've never felt before, I can't explain it and it's terrifying because he has awakened a darkness inside me that I know will never go back to sleep. And I don't want it to, I want more, I crave more. I want to see how far we can push each other, find our limits and then break through them.

Sitting up, I wince, my body aching from last night. I can't believe everything that happened. The knife, Ronan taking me from behind, the balcony. I passed out while we had sex on the balcony and I don't remember coming or him bringing me to the bed. Yet here I am. I'm naked, but I feel clean and I smell like the hotel's lotion, which I didn't put on last night. I look around the room, a gasp escaping me when I see the body is gone. There's no blood, no body, no Ronan. Anxiety fills me as I climb out of bed, stumbling around. His bag is gone.

Turning to the mattress, I see clothes folded neatly with a small paper wrapped bouquet. Looking at the flowers, I notice the soft white petals as they turn downward in a tear or bell shape. They're so sad, yet beautiful. Bringing them to my nose, I inhale deeply, allowing the green, spring scent to consume me before putting them down and picking up the clothes. I slip into the high waisted jeans and cropped tank before sliding on the plaid overshirt.

"Really?" I chuckle, looking at the shoes on the floor. "You know my shoe size? Do I even want to know how he figured that out?"

"A ruler,"

"FFFFUCK!" I shriek at Ronan's voice as I stumble back onto the bed. He raises a dark blond brow as a smirk plays on his face.

"You alright there, Angel?" He teases before handing me a bag. "Breakfast," he replies to my questioning stare.

"You got me breakfast?" I ask as he hands me a coffee. "Where's the—"

"Eat up," he interrupts. "We're heading out in ten minutes."

"Where are we going?" I ask as he taps something out on his phone.

"Gotta get moving," he sighs as he slips his phone into his pants pocket. "I need to get across the border, I've already been here longer than I should've."

"Wait, am I going with you?" I ask with a piece of a donut

hanging out of my mouth. Ronan looks at the pastry and a genuine smile forms on his face as he crouches in front of me and leans in, biting off the end of the donut.

"I gave you your out last night, Angel." His hand snakes behind my neck, gripping me into place. "You chose to stay here and let me fuck you into unconsciousness over a balcony. You're mine now, and forever." His lips are mere millimeters from mine and I'm sure he can hear the quickening of my heart rate and my breathing.

"And when you get tired of me?" I whisper against his mouth. "What happens then?"

"Impossible," he states as if what I'm saying is the most preposterous thing ever spoken.

"Right," I say with a chuckle. "Like I haven't heard that before." Giggling, I tap his nose before going to stand. Ronan grips my wrist and pulls me to him.

"Everly." His voice is low and full of desire as he breathes out my name as if he owns me… then again, maybe he does. "I've been watching you with a deadly hunger, obsessively studying every breath, every move. My addiction to you is not just a gentle flame, it's an inferno of desire that devours my very sanity. I've imagined countless scenarios where you're mine and mine alone, where we're the only souls left in existence. Everly, you may think you have control over your own life, but my sweet angel, you couldn't be more wrong. We are woven into each other's very beings, there is no escape from us. Even in death, we will be intertwined with each other. I need you to understand, there is no getting tired of you. You are mine, you always were meant to be mine, and you will always be mine. One way or another, you will belong to me, forever. Nothing will stand in the way of that— not even you."

"Not even me?" I question weakly, my heart pounding in my ears as I lose myself in his gaze.

"If you try to leave me," he murmurs, his lips connecting with mine so softly it causes me to whimper. "I will kill you, and then I will kill myself and come find you again." I open my mouth in shock and he takes it as an invitation, forcing his tongue into my mouth, claiming it as his.

"Ronan," I pant as he climbs on top of me, his hot mouth planting feverish kisses over my neck and jawline. "Ronan, how am I going with you if you're crossing the border?" He freezes and pulls back.

"You're going to sit in the front seat like the good girl you are and when they ask for your passport, you'll give it to them."

"I-I don't have a passport, plus won't it look weird, a Canadian bringing back an American?" Annoyed, he pushes himself off me and adjusts his erection pushing at his jeans before walking over to his bag.

"I'm from Boston, I'm not Canadian. Not too good with accents are ya?" he teases, causing me to blush.

"I don't know. I've been in the midwest my whole life, I figured you're just what they sound like up there. That doesn't answer my question though, I don't have a passport."

"I have a guy who got me the proper documents. We are going to meet him tonight to get yours."

"I don't know," I whisper, biting on my nail. "Ronan, going to another country…if I'm caught, they'll send me to jail."

"First, do you think I would allow that to happen? And second, what do you mean you don't know? What's there to know? You *are* getting in my car and we *are* going across the border." His voice is dark and commanding in a way I haven't heard since being tied in the woods, blindfolded and pleading with him.

"What if I say no," I whisper as he shrugs his bag on his shoulder. "What if I want to stay here?" He turns and looks me over, the backs of his fingers running over my cheek.

"I told you, Everly, you belong with me, forever. I won't live without you. I gave you an out last night and you chose this."

"Yeah? And? Ronan, you wanted to die last night!"

"So what?" His voice cracks ever so slightly as his hand drops from my face. I watch his brows furrow in confusion and his eyes look almost lost. "You said those things to me so I wouldn't die?" I open my mouth to lie, to tell him that I didn't mean it that way. But… I did. I talked him down because the thought of him dying and leaving me to clean the mess… it was too much.

I'm silent for too long and he sees the truth written over my face.

"Right," he whispers, looking away. "Can't love a monster."

"Ronan! That's not fair! You took me! Nothing about this, about us is normal, I can't fall in love with you! I'm still not sure I trust you won't murder me! What we're doing, yeah it's enjoyable, but sustainable? Really? So I go to Canada and we go on a killing spree there? When does it stop? You and I will end up in prison or killing each other. How am I supposed to sleep next to you at night and not fear your addiction taking hold and you ending me?"

"I don't kill there," he hisses as if I've insulted him. "I kill once a year, until now. This is new for me too, alright! I didn't expect this and I'm not sure where it's going to lead us but what am I supposed to do? You and I can't be apart. And between the two of us, you're the only one who has contemplated murdering me in my sleep." I wince at his truthful words.

"Ronan, as much as I am enjoying this, it's becoming very clear that I need to go. You and I... I think we're addicted to this and no good can come of it." I say, getting up and walking toward the door.

"I'm sorry." He laughs darkly. "Did I give you some impression that you're allowed to leave without me?" I turn to glare back at him but the hurt and betrayal in his eyes breaks me. He's trying to mask it but I see the panic, it's the same panic I saw when he thought I was going to jump in that guy's car. Reaching up, I cup his cheek, and he flinches as though I might strike him.

"Ro—"

"No," he grits out, jerking his face away. "If you are leaving me, if you're going to go on with your life and forget about me... about us, then you let that name die."

"This is toxic," I try to get him to look at me but he refuses, his eyes burning holes in the carpet. "You know what is happening between us—it's wrong, it's a sick and twisted addiction. I know this because even as I'm saying this, my body wants to stay here and find out how much more twisted we can become. It's not safe, for either of us. We will be what ends the other."

"You're right," he whispers, his eyes finally reaching mine. He looks so lost. "But I'm okay with you being my undoing, my end. Your body wants to stay with me, but my fucking soul can't imagine being ripped from yours. This isn't just fucking, Everly, I'll chop my cock off and give it to you if that's what you ask. You are my oxygen, if you leave, I will die."

"We've known each other less than a week," I manage out, my heart aching for the panicked man in front of me. He looks so frightened and alone.

"In this life maybe." He drops to his knees in front of me. "Everly, you and I have done all of this before, I know you know that because you feel it too. You heard me begging you. You feel me. We are—"

"If you want me to go with you," I say firmly, though my body trembles, I can't listen to him. I can't because everything he's saying is in my head already. We are connected, soulmates, or two halves of the same twisted, depraved soul. I need him like I need my next breath. But no one should feel that kind of awakening after a week—soulmates or not. Inhaling, I steel my gaze as I look into his pleading one. "If you want me to go, you will have to take me in a body bag. I'm not going alive."

"Why?" His voice breaks as a tear rolls down his face. "W-Why are you doing this? I'll protect you. I-I will give you anything you want! Money? Jewelry? A house? A car? My fucking heart on a platter? Anything, just name it and it's yours!" He's frantic as he reaches for me but I back away.

"Freedom," I whisper. "Freedom to make my own choice." His lip quivers for a moment as he looks me over.

"Angel, you will make the wrong choice."

"It's my wrong choice to make." I counter as he shakes his head while standing up.

"Why can't you see that I'm trying to protect you," He takes a step toward me and I step back, until I'm at the door.

"I know you think you are," I say softly. "But the only thing that I need protecting from right now, is you." It's as if I stabbed him with my words. His face scrunches up as he closes his eyes, his body deflating. I take the opportunity to reach into his pocket and grab his phone before opening the hotel room door. Ronan grabs me by my hair and tries to tug me back.

"You're not leaving me." He grits out through clenched teeth. "I'm not living without you."

"Let me go," I whisper calmly. "Or I will scream." The door is open and all I'd have to do is yell for help and it would all be over.

"You wouldn't," he breathes out, "You scream and they will take me away." I shake my head.

"Don't make me," I beg, stepping over the threshold as his hold on my hair releases. "I'm so sorry," I whisper as he continues to stare through me.

"You will be;" He promises before shutting the door, leaving me standing in the hall. I look down at his phone, it's locked, of course. Sighing, I make my way to the lobby. I don't know what I'm going to do, but I know I have to get as far away from Ronan as I can before I change my mind.

ronan

CHAPTER 7

She left.

I stare at my tablet screen while sitting in my car. She's been picked up by someone judging by how fast she's moving now. Honestly, I can't believe she took my phone. It's the easiest fucking thing to track. I'm glad she did though, because right now, I'm in no state to be trying to locate her any other way.

She left.

"Fuck," I hiss out as the blade runs across my arm. I can't remember the last time I needed this kind of release. Probably over a decade. But here I am, line after line, trying like hell to numb the pain. How could she leave? I worship her. I understand her. She and I are on a spiritual level that we won't find anywhere else and she just decided, what? That I'm too much? That I'm too unhinged? She brings a stranger into our hotel to send me into a jealous rage but I am the unhinged one?

Staring at the screen, I light a cigarette while trying to ignore the burning in my eyes. I cried. I don't cry. I haven't since one of the first times my father rammed his cock down my throat.

But I did cry when she left. I feel as though I can't breathe. I know it's only been a week, I know it's fast, but what am I supposed to do? Deny what's happened? That I've fallen over the edge for her? Pretend like she and I aren't soulmates until a respectable amount of time goes by? Fuck that. I'm a grown ass man and I know what I'm feeling and I've never been into societal norms.

She's so sorry.

Sorry—fucking wonderful. Sorry is perfect. Sorry is great. Please Everly, be sooo fucking sorry. So sorry for walking into my life and giving me hope for the first time in my fucking life just to rip it away. I felt seen, I felt able to breathe and she… well, she's sorry. So mother fucking sorry. She will be, if she thinks I'll just tuck my tail between my legs and leave, she's wrong. I will follow her to the ends of this world and the next. I will be in the shadows, watching. What? She expects to go on and live a *normal* life? She expects to date? Fuckkk my angel isn't that stupid is she? Certainly not. She has to know I'll kill every one of them. And if she doesn't know, she will when she notices none of them seem to come around after the first date. I will burn this world, Heaven and Hell down for her. But in the same breath, I will burn *her* world as well. Nothing about my love for her is selfless or giving. It's possessive, dark and all-consuming. And I'll stop at nothing to keep her as mine and only mine.

Tapping on the screen, I unlock my phone from my tablet and turn on the microphone so I can hear what's happening wherever she is. I hear the loud truck engine, she must be in a semi, fucking wonderful. I don't hear any talking as I continue to drag my blade over my arm again.

It's insulting that she seems to ignore how deep my devotion, my obsession for her runs. It's also insulting that she pretends to fear the idea of us more than a fucking over the road trucker. I mean, I adore her but this here is *precisely* why I cannot allow her to be on her own. She's in a semi-truck and she's under the impression that I'm truly going to turn my back on her and move on. What do I need to do to get her to realize that there's no going back. I will never be the man I was and I'm okay with it as long as I have her, without her… well, I'm here, seeking relief and obsessing.

Obsession is a double-edged sword, slicing through my sanity and leading me down a path of self-destruction. The more I fixate on my desires, on her, the deeper this blade cuts into my soul, leaving behind a trail of destruction and despair. My obsession with Everly consumes me completely and it will for eternity. I will give her anything, I will do anything for her. Except let her go. I refuse to give her that. If she's gone, then… what am I? Who am I? I can't go through another day, hour, minute, second with her being away from me. It can't work this way and I don't know how I am going to get her to realize that I need her, I need her more than I need anything. My heart beats only for her. She can think what she wants, she can be afraid of her mutual obsession for me, that's fine, I'll allow it. But she will do it while beside me.

I exhale my pull from my cigarette as I stare at the tracker. It doesn't take long for me to figure out whose truck she's in once I hear the driver call in on their radio. A simple— illegal—search from an acquaintance and I've found his CDL, the license plate on his truck and *oh that's interesting*—his next scheduled stop is a truckstop owned by someone with his last name. Why would he schedule a stop like that?

"Where are we going?" Everly's voice is a punch in the

chest. She sounds scared, and her voice is watery. Had… had
he—

"No," I snap, my head shaking back and forth. "No, no, no,
no." I can't, I can't think that. If I do, I'll kill everyone and
burn every city until I get to her.

"Shut your whore ass up," he grunts and I take a steadying
breath as I put my car in drive and take off down the highway.
They're ten miles ahead of me and I need to be calm as I
approach the truck. I can't rush out there, he could have a gun
on Everly and I wouldn't be able to get to her before he shot
her.

"Fuck you," Everly spits back as an angry sob wrecks
through her. It both destroys me and makes me proud to know
she's still fighting. "I swear to god if you don't let me out I will
kill you."

There's the skin slapping skin before the driver—*Bucky
Reynolds* grits out, "I'm going to take personal pleasure in
knowing that once I get you to the stop, the rest of your life
will be spent knowing that I fucked your little ass until you
vomited from the pain." I nearly lose my hearing and vision at
the rage building inside me as I press down on the accelerator.

"Fuck!" I scream, punching my steering wheel as I will
my car to go faster. I'm cutting him apart, slowly, so he feels
everything. I'm going to force him to eat his own intestines
and choke on his dick.

"Yeah," I hear her spit and I'm assuming it lands on his
face. *Angel, I love your fearlessness but not when I'm not
there to stop him.* "Well, I'm going to take personal pleasure
in knowing that no matter what happens to me, my big, mean,
scary boyfriend will stop at nothing to find you, and he will
rip your heart out and make you eat it." *Her…boyfriend?* I rub

my chest as an odd sensation wraps itself around my heart and squeezes.

"Yeah?" He huffs and I hear him putting his truck into park. "And where's your big scary boyfriend now, huh?"

I'm five minutes out, and when I get there, it's going to be a fucking blood bath.

Everly

CHAPTER 8

"Get off me!" I scream as *Bucky* the filthy asshole trucker drags me by my hair around the back of this run-the-fuck-down truck stop. I don't think I'm supposed to make it out of here alive. Bucky tosses me into the back room, using his boot to shove my back, making me fall forward on an open tool box. I hiss in pain as the corner slices my palm.

"Shoo wee!" he calls loudly while gripping my hair again and yanking me to my feet. "I don't know about you, Sweetheart, but I've been looking forward to bustin' this ass since I watched you bouncing it down the highway."

"Get. Off!" I grit out while trying to elbow him. He blocks me while unfastening my jeans.

"Oh, I'm about to." I gag at his voice as he shoves me to the floor. Ronan's phone falls from my pocket and I notice that, unlike before, the screen isn't locked. And there's a green light on the top. Is… Is Ronan tracking me? Is he listening?

"Ronan," I whisper as I hear Bucky removing his belt. "I'm

sorry. Just know, this was not your fault. I don't blame you, and you're not a monster."

"Are you saying your prayers there, Sweetheart?" Bucky chuckles as he gets to his knees. "Because God ain't saving you this time." He leans over and I know it's now or never.

"I know," I whisper before rolling over onto my back. "I'm saving myself," gripping the chisel I grabbed out of the tool box, I drive it into the side of his neck. He begins to sputter as blood shoots out. It takes everything in me but I grip the chisel's handle tightly as I drag it across his throat, slicing it open and bathing me in his blood.

Bucky's lifeless body collapses on top of me and I instantly wiggle free before scooting myself back against a wall, bringing my knees to my chest. I'm mildly aware of Ronan's phone vibrating, but I don't reach for it. I can't, my body is frozen, as if in shock, even though my mind is racing. Every single thought racing through my head and not one is regret. Well not regret for this. Regret for leaving Ronan though, god I have so much regret for that. I should've stayed, should've dropped to my knees and told him the truth. That I wasn't scared of him or his darkness, but I was scared of getting in deeper, and losing him.

The door flies open and I know it's Ronan; I don't have to look, I can feel his overwhelming presence.

"Oh my god," he breathes out as he rushes to me. I notice he places his gun on the floor behind. His hands go to touch me but he pulls back, as if in fear. His eyes scan me frantically. "Where are you hurt?" he manages and I finally look up at him, cocking my head to one side. *Hurt?* I hold my sliced palm up, noting it's covered in drying blood. I had no idea blood could dry so fast. Though maybe it's been a while? How long have I been sitting here?

"Everly!" Ronan's desperate voice pulls me out of my haze as his hands grip my face. "Angel, w-what… are you hurt?" I shake my head slowly as my eyes travel to Bucky, he's face down in a pool of blood.

"I…" My voice sounds so far away, like I'm hearing myself talk in another room. "Didn't—there was no knife. I-I couldn't twist," I whisper, staring up at him as the burning sensation hits my eyes. "I couldn't twist," I say again as it all begins to hit me. "Oh my god, I slit his…he bled… so much, Ronan." My bottom lip wobbles as I stare at him. I'm not staring at Ronan the serial killer though. There is so much fear, worry and love in his face, in his stare. And it's all directed at me.

"Everly, baby, you're in shock." *Am I? No I can't be. My brain is working. I mean my body isn't listening but…*

Ronan pulls me to his chest and it's now I realize I'm sobbing. When did I start crying? Why am I crying? What is happening to me?

"Hey, Pops," a male voice drawls as he walks into the back. "Hurry up with the bitch, I gotta ship her to—" He stops talking when he sees the gory scene before him and Ronan's pointed suppressed pistol at him.

"Ship who?" Ronan growls, standing up and pulling me behind him. The guy, maybe my age, clears his throat as he looks at Bucky's dead body again.

"You killed my father?" He whispers in disbelief.

"He was trying to rape me!" I shout, startling both men.

"So you fucking slaughter him like a hog?! Look at you, you fucking freak!" *Look at me?* I look down at all the blood covering me, my clothes, my hair, the shoes Ronan got me.

"Oh no," I breathe out. "M-My new shoes!" a whimper

escapes me as I look apologetically to Ronan. "I'm so sorry."

"Angel, I'll buy you as many pairs as you want later but now isn't the best time." He gestures to his gun and the guy.

"You fucking psychotic bit—" I gasp and cover my mouth as the bullet enters the man's head, exiting and spattering on the door behind him.

"I oughta shoot him again, fucker, calling you that." Ronan growls before turning back to me. "Are you with me, Angel?"

Are you with me? Not 'are you okay'. He knows that's a stupid question. But am I with him? I think back through everything. There's no going back, there's no escaping him and there's no running from this. Do I really want to run? I did run but the entire time I hoped he was coming for me. Leaving him is not an option, my addiction to him running deeper than any logical thought or warning. Like a moth drawn to an alluring flame, I crave his presence and the intense heat that comes with it. Our union may be dangerous, like setting fire to gasoline, but I embrace the flames and am willing to burn within them as long as we burn together. Yes, I am irrevocably intertwined with him in every imaginable way, unable to break free from this passionate inferno we've created.

"Yes," I whisper as I step toward him slowly. He watches me as if he's waiting for me to freak out or bolt. I do neither, instead I jump into his arms, wrapping my legs around his waist as my tongue plunges into his mouth. He growls, accepting my advances while slamming me into a wall before breaking the kiss. My hazy eyes look over him, his lips and mouth are smeared with Bucky's blood. An odd compulsion comes over me as I put my thumbs on either side of his mouth and trail them upwards, causing the blood to form red lines, looking like a smile. His brows furrow and I release a laugh. It's a small giggle at first but soon turns into a full-on cackle, it's not the smile that is making me laugh, no, it's that in the short time we've been together, through all the pain, murder, fear... through all of it, I've come out the other side, feeling more alive than ever. This man, this serial killer has awaken a side of me I didn't know existed, and instead of me feeling shame or disgust, I feel happy... free.

"I'm a monster," I whisper against his mouth.

"You are," he purrs while dragging his tongue up my chin and lips. "But so am I." I giggle before sucking on his tongue.

"I killed a man,"

"You did." He kisses the tip of my nose.

"And I have another I want to kill." He lets out a breathy chuckle.

"Easy there my love. Let's get the blood of your first off before you run to your next."

"Fuck me," I groan while grinding against him. He rolls his eyes in pleasure as he lowers me to remove my pants. He lifts me back up while freeing his hard dick before slamming it into me.

"Ohhh...now there's a pretty noise." He grunts while thrusting into me again. I'm frantic as I rip off our blood-stained clothes, our bodies covered in Bucky's blood.

"Harder," I rasp as his hand goes to my throat. "Ronan," I whisper as I feel myself coming around his cock.

"You're so perfect." He whimpers out as he continues to thrust into me over and over again. "My perfect angel, so fucking beautiful. My soulmate... baby I'm going to come in you and you're never leaving me again, do you understand me?" I nod over and over. This apparently irritates him because he thrusts deeper into me and holds me there, while staring into my eyes.

"Do. You. Understand. Me?" His voice is a low and feral tone that I feel in my core.

"Yes," I whimper. "I'm never leaving. I love you, Ronan." I pant as he starts thrusting again. My words cause his movements to halt. He stares at me, jaw slack.

"What?" He breathes out, and I notice he looks almost afraid of my response.

"I said," I whine as I buck against him while kissing his lips. "I love you, Ronan." His lips consume mine as he thrusts into me again, and again, and again. I try to move away to scream as I come again but Ronan grips me tighter, consuming my cries while allowing me to absorb his as we come together sealing this bond between us. This bond it's unbreakable, sealed in the blood of our victim and fueled by a burning desire for more. More kills, more highs, more of each other. Just more. And I will never stop wanting, yearning, craving more of him and the life he's presented to me. And I know that he too is wanting the same thing.

RONAN

EPILOGUE

<u>One Year Later</u>

Everly's eyes bore into mine, her irises reflecting a twisted mirror of my own madness and insatiable desire. It's as if we are two halves of the same depraved soul, bound together by an unbreakable bond of mutual obsession.

"Are you ready?" she squeals out, her body nearly vibrating. She's so beautiful when she's excited like this. I haven't seen it in so long. She's been so happy over the last year, and… so have I.

After the clean up at the truck stop, I made a call to a friend in Oregon who helped us dispose of the bodies and her friend got us a passport for Everly. She and I crossed the border and six months later, we were married. Everly has thrived in our house. She spends her days working at a local coffee shop and evenings are spent with me. Some nights are dark and demented; I'll chase her through the woods, setting up traps and fucking her senseless once she's caught. Other nights, well, we watch television, make dinner together, cuddle even. It's a side I've never experienced before and honestly, it scared the shit out of me the first couple of times. But now, I crave those nights almost as much as well, these trips.

"You fucking bitch!" Devon screams as he fights against his cuffs. We're in an old abandoned barn on the outskirts of east Colorado. As a rule, I never visit the same area twice and after the absolute rampage she and I went on, I was ready to start going toward Florida for hunts. But what can I say, she has me wrapped around her delicate little finger and what my angel wants, she gets. And she wanted one last kill in Colorado.

"Hey," I warn slowly as I sit on a stool. "That's no way to speak to a lady." Everly giggles brightly, her nose wrinkling from her large smile as she walks over to the table where my tools are.

"So many decisions," she hums while looking at the different instruments. Spinning on the balls of her feet she looks at Devon. "You have no idea how excited I am that we were able to get together this weekend!"

"You're fucking insane Pip!" He spits out causing her to flinch. I stay still, I'm not to move unless she gives me the word. This is *her* moment. Not mine.

"Ya know," She taps a pair of cutters to her plush lips as she strolls up to him. "I hate that name," she growls. As she takes the cutters and…

"Jesus Christ," I mutter as she snips the man's nipple off. He starts thrashing and screaming as she drops the nipple on the table before walking back.

"You fucking cunt!" He slobbers through his tears and I release a low growl while shifting. Everly looks over to me, her magical eyes bright and excited.

"Love you." She blows me a kiss and it has a cooling effect over my entire body.

"I love you too." And fuck do I mean it. I love her so fucking much. Our love is not for the faint of heart. It's a twisted tango, fueled by vengeance and held together by our insatiable thirst for each other. Our burning flames for each other will never burn out, only growing larger and hotter with each passing second. I'm addicted to everything that makes up Everly Kipling and the fact that she shares the same obsession, the same need, it tells me that we will only grow closer as time goes on.

Everly grabs a knife and walks over to Devon, and I have to fight the moan I feel watching my wife carve into her abuser's flesh. She's so beautiful—so brave and confident.

"Fuckkk," I moan, grabbing the crotch of my pants as she bends over to cut his Achilles tendon.

"Like that?" She purrs over Devon's wails. She saunters over to me, straddling my lap as my mouth instantly goes to her exposed cleavage. She giggles and smacks my arm. "You know the rules. You can watch and touch yourself all you want. But you don't get me until his heart stops beating."

"Angel," My gravelly voice breathes out. "Baby, I can fix that heartbeat in two seconds, make no mistake."

"But you won't," She warns before walking over to Devon and wrapping a blindfold around his head. "Sorry, as much as I want to watch the light leave your eyes, this is a special day for Ronan and me, and I have a surprise for him that you don't get to see." I raise my brow as she turns back to me. "It was a year ago today that you took me from that coffee shop." I smirk, running my thumb over my lip.

"Is it? I had no idea." I chuckle as she smiles.

"So I thought what better way to celebrate than to have a little fun."

"Isn't that what we're doing?" I question, gesturing to the hanging man.

She shrugs. "A little more fun, like... oh I don't know..." She unzips her jacket and removes her pants, leaving her in a very sheer green bra and thong.

"Oh my god," I marvel, my cock growing hard instantly.

"You can call me Everly." She winks as she bends all the fucking way over to grab something out of the duffel bag. She's bent so far over I'm staring right at those plump, glistening pussy lips that are about to make me fall to my fucking knees.

"Everly," I breathe out my needy whimper while palming myself through my pants. "Angel... fuck." She giggles as she walks over to me, leans over and licks my lips.

"Let me see how much you enjoy the show," she purrs, her pupils dilated and her smile devious. She backs away as I lean back on the stool, unzipping my jeans and freeing my cock.

"Yay!" She claps before spinning back to Devon. "Alright, let's get this show on the road! I've got a beach vacation in my future and I don't want this impeding on it." She trails the tip of her blade across Devon's chest and around to his back as she strolls around him. Devon screams in agony, but it only serves as background music as I watch my sexy wife swing her sinful hips with each step. She reaches up, stabbing Devon in the side and I smile as she expertly twists the blade before pulling it out. Blood splatters across her body and I groan as my hand fists my cock.

She runs her hands over her large breasts and down her flat stomach as Devon's blood smears everywhere. She's a work of fucking art.

"Harder," she demands, pointing her blade and my cock. I spit in my hand before doing as I'm told.

"Everly," I moan as I squeeze the base.

"You both are sick!" Devon weakly cries, he won't last long with that open wound.

"Are we?" Everly questions innocently. "Funny I remember saying the same thing to you and your buddies when you raped me. I remember begging you to leave me alone when you forced me to live with you so you could continue your abuse. What was it you called me? Walking Sex?" Her chuckle is dark. "I may be sick, but so are you."

"I…" He spits blood from his mouth. "I took pity on you. You stupid slut, you're only good at one thing, and that's spreading your legs. Figured it would be easier to have you at my disposal." I stop stroking—I'm about to either blow my load or murder him myself and I don't like being so far opposite in my head.

"Well, just so you know." Everly holds the blade to Devon's throat. "Not once were those orgasms real." She runs the knife across his throat, blood pouring from him as he sputters before shaking and finally going still.

Everly walks over to me, her perfect body dripping in his blood. She says nothing as she sits on my lap, impaling herself with my cock. I'm about to speak when she puts the blade to my throat, her gaze dark and hazy, high from the kill. "I could kill you too," she whispers while grinding against me.

"You could," I pant, feeling my orgasm build.

"It would be so fast, you'd never be able to s-stop me." Her head rolls back as she moans out.

"Not too fast I hope." My breaths become ragged as I reach in my pocket and pull out my blade, pressing it against her throat. "I would like us to go out together."

She smirks before tossing her knife aside, I do the same as her mouth consumes mine. Growling, I hoist her up, and walk to the table, I swipe everything off, causing it to clatter to the floor before dropping her on it and driving deeper into her.

"Ronan!" Her cry is breathless as I press her thighs open wider while pounding deep into her—blood covering us both, deepening the dark bond between us as we come together in a feral tangle of screams, scratches and grunts.

"I love you," I grunt between my rapid thrusts as I fill her needy cunt. "I fucking love you, Everly, fuck!" I grip her hips as I ram into her one last time.

Everly pulls me to her, kissing me softly. "I love you, too." She smiles softly. "Now, I think I was promised a trip to the beach?" I bow my head, chuckling softly.

"Yes, well, I think we got a bit of a clean-up to do first." I laugh at her pout before kissing her again. "Come on, help me out and then I'll give you a shower."

The End

Printed in Great Britain
by Amazon